PISTIS

THE THIRD ELEMENT

THE QUEST

TERRANCE R SOLTOW

A wholly owned subsidiary of TBN

Pistis the Third Element, Volume 1: The Quest
Trilogy Christian Publishers A Wholly Owned Subsidiary of Trinity Broadcasting Network
2442 Michelle Drive Tustin, CA 92780
Copyright © 2023 by Terrance R. Soltow
Scripture quotations marked BST are from The English translation of The Septuagint by Sir Lancelot Charles Lee Brenton (1851). Public domain.
Scripture quotations marked CJB are taken from the Complete Jewish Bible, Copyright ©1998 and 2016 by David H. Stern. Used by permission. All rights reserved worldwide. Scripture quotations marked NIV are taken from the Holy Bible, New International Version®, NIV®. Copyright © 1973, 1978, 1984, 2011 by Biblica, Inc.TM. Used by permission of Zondervan. All rights reserved worldwide. www.zondervan.com. The "NIV" and "New International Version" are trademarks registered in the United States Patent and Trademark Office by Biblica, Inc. Scripture taken from the New King James Version®. Copyright © 1982 by Thomas Nelson. Used by permission. All rights reserved. Scripture quotations marked NRSV are taken from the New Revised Standard Version Bible, copyright © 1989 National Council of the Churches of Christ in the United States of America. Used by permission. All rights reserved. Scripture quotations marked KJV are taken from the King James Version of the Bible. Public domain.
No part of this book may be reproduced, stored in a retrieval system, or transmitted by any means without written permission from the author. All rights reserved. Printed in the USA.
Rights Department, 2442 Michelle Drive, Tustin, CA 92780.
Trilogy Christian Publishing/TBN and colophon are trademarks of Trinity Broadcasting Network.
Cover design by: Trilogy
For information about special discounts for bulk purchases, please contact Trilogy Christian Publishing.
Trilogy Disclaimer: The views and content expressed in this book are those of the author and may not necessarily reflect the views and doctrine of Trilogy Christian Publishing or the Trinity Broadcasting Network.
Manufactured in the United States of America
10 9 8 7 6 5 4 3 2 1
Library of Congress Cataloging-in-Publication Data is available.
ISBN: 979-8-89041-268-3
E-ISBN: 979-8-89041-269-0

Table of Contents

Introduction. 7

My Believer Is Broken 9

The Straw That Broke the Camel's Back 35

Lost, Not Broken. 43

The Quest 59

Evidence 73

Search for the Sword. 89

What Is in a Name?. 109

The Last Shall Be First 133

The Word of God 157

Choice. 179

Follow Where It Leads 197

Introduction

This is a fictional story; do not forget that. While it is fictional, it also contains truths. I leave it up to you, the reader, to figure out what is and what isn't true. The path to determining truth or fiction is strewn with a great many obstacles. Perhaps the greatest barrier to truth is tradition. Not all tradition represents truth, and not all traditions are false.

I wish you success as you travel with the main character, Brea Rea Joyce.

CHAPTER 1

MY BELIEVER IS BROKEN

Let me introduce myself: my name is Brea Rea Joyce (Rea is pronounced "REE"; my parent's sense of humor, I always thought). I'm an archeologist currently living in Chicago. What brought me to Chicago? I came to the city to work with an organization that recovers sunken ships from the chilly waters of Lake Michigan.

I grew up in southern Wisconsin, in the little town of Clinton, just north of the Illinois border. It was a great little town to grow up in; everyone knew everyone else. The bad thing is everyone knew everyone else's business. We moved from there to Beloit, Wisconsin, when I was nine. Things changed a lot, moving from a small town to a larger city. The move and the reasons for it caused a significant stressor in my life; I survived, but not without scars.

I received my degree in archeology from a private

university in Wisconsin. A few years ago, I set out on a very strange adventure. It was more of a quest than an adventure, or perhaps both. I'll explain more as we continue this conversation.

To help you understand what prompted my quest, I would like to share the stories of several people who have struggled with the same issue I dealt with, a condition that seemed to leave us with an inability to believe. My story falls among the ones I am sharing. All names have been altered to ensure privacy.

I hesitate to tell you which story is mine. Why? Well, let's just say I want to leave this open to your imagination. Chances are you will determine what caused my brokenness based on what may be your own. Each story represents a life situation that left these people with the same condition I had, a condition I called a *broken believer*; each of us with this issue was conditioned by life events that caused us to demand clear proof of certain things before believing. Simple things may not require much proof; however, the major things in our lives, such as "Is there a God?" require something more. Much more.

To accept things as true without evidence and to believe those things, many call faith. Unfortunately, for a great many of us, the ability to meet this requirement is impossible. The ability some seem to be in possession of that allows them to accept things without proof is either broken or nonexistent in us as broken believers.

My Believer Is Broken

Let me introduce you to some of the people in my life who have shared their stories with me and asked if I would include them in this book. Their hope is that you might better understand our plight. Should you happen to cross someone who says, "I just can't believe!" Perhaps this book will provide you with the message they need. To this end, I share their stories and mine.

Carroll

"In my case, with my friends, what I did not realize at the time, was a program running that said, 'They are just going to let you down, and that will hurt. Don't let that happen; hurt them before they get a chance to hurt you.' As a result, I would sabotage every relationship. When it would be ruined, my subconscious program would be satisfied that it had performed well and move on to the next victim. Sadly, the conscious mind, unaware of what was going on, would see things differently; it would say, 'I can't trust anyone to be my friend; look how it always ends.' After a period, relationships would end faster than the one before unless, of course, the individual had the endurance of a saint; then, it might continue a little longer. However, that thing inside would eventually succeed and ruin that relationship as well. Sadly, this case scenario was not limited to friends only.

It also happened with family members, which probably explains a lot of ruined families. This pattern left a great many relationships in a heap of brokenness in my life. My actions fed my doubt about people, and believing in anyone or anything became impossible for me."

David

"My parents divorced when I was eight. My mother was constantly breaking her promises to me, never showing up, always having some flimsy excuse as to why she couldn't pick me up and spend time with me, and it left scars. Don't get me wrong, I love her. However, as time went on, I began to doubt everything. After all, when you can't trust the one person you should be able to trust, your mother, how can you trust anyone or anything else? Something inside of me seemed to be broken. It is not that I didn't want to believe; I simply could not. My ability to believe was somehow broken."

Susan

"When my parent's marriage ended, Dad remarried. My stepmom loves me, and I am grateful for her influence in my life, but something seemed to be holding me back from *fully appreciating her. There are a lot of things that are involved in a relationship between a stepparent and the stepchild, things that, typically, neither of them understands. What stood between us, as I look back, I'm sure, was an inner thing, a fidelity a child feels for their biological parents, even when one or both leaves the child behind. Because of that step-relationship struggle, many are left broken and thinking that believing in people or things becomes impossible; there is this something inside, something most of us don't even realize is there; perhaps a still, small voice saying, 'Don't trust, don't believe; it will only leave you more broken.' As a result, you build walls that protect you from getting hurt. After a time, your ability to believe is broken, and you simply cannot believe."*

Steven

"Due to emotional issues and drug use in my home, I was removed and put in foster care. I cannot explain why, but I felt my parents' problems were my fault. I acted up in ways that caused several foster parents to ask for me to be removed from their homes. In school, I had issues with friends; I never understood what was happening. Something inside of me kept telling me I was awful and no one liked me. I couldn't see what was happening; no one wanted to be around me. I stopped believing anyone or anything."

Let me pause for a moment and share something many are not aware of. Each of us has or has had emotional scars, with some open wounds, perhaps. Please understand I am not talking about just those in these stories, but rather all human beings. These scars and or wounds reside deep within our being, in a place that dictates our actions. Some think this place is our subconscious; however, there is something deeper than our subconscious that sets the stage for the programs our subconscious automatically runs.

Only now is science beginning to realize this deeper layer that plays out like this. First is the surface layer, the conscious mind. It is generally agreed that our conscious self is rather primitive. Some say the conscious mind can process approximately *40 bits* of information per second; they say the subconscious, the second layer, on the other hand, can process between 11,000,000 and *20,000,000 (20 million) bits* of information in that same second. If you and I were to visualize this contrast, the subconscious watching the conscious mind work is like us sitting around watching a tree grow; the time it takes for the process is so slow we become bored and move on, stopping, occasionally, over the years to note the changes in the tree. The subconscious becomes easily bored with the slow activity of the conscious and starts off in different directions, running multiple activities, considering, and processing several different ideas and thoughts while the conscious mind is trying to determine if a thing is blue or purple. This is probably why, occasionally, when we are talking or telling someone something, we lose track of what we are saying. When older people have this happen, some attribute it to old age or disease. However, I wonder if it isn't the subconscious moving on, and when it does, the conscious gets lost. That's just my theory.

Occasionally, especially during trauma or stress, the conscious mind is forced to focus on a particular thing. It's illuminated or becomes tuned into something very deep. The result, the conscious is enlightened. These moments of inspiration have produced incredible results.

According to some, within our subconscious, there are programs that run. Our conscious mind seldom thinks about these actions or programs. For example, your heart is beating; what makes that happen? It is a program within the subconscious. Perhaps you're performing a routine task, and at first, that task took conscious effort to perform; however, after repeating the task several times, you can do it without thinking about it because the subconscious has developed a program that runs in the background of the conscious, allowing the primitive limited conscious mind to focus on other things. When it comes to our daily lives, the subconscious programs are written and control our actions without us giving conscious thought to why we do them. Many of these actions are beneficial, such as breathing;

however, some of the programs cause us incredible pain, confusion, and frustration.

As I said earlier, there is another controlling layer; this is where things get a little strange. Many think that there are only two things controlling us, the conscious and the subconscious; however, the subconscious is not the core. Think of the subconscious as the computer, running reactionary programs without conscious thought. The conscious is the monitor displaying what the subconscious program dictates; however, you must answer a question: Who is the programmer? Few of us pause to consider the answer to this. The programmer is a very powerful part of us; some call it the heart.

Most think of the heart as that internal organ that pumps blood; however, some in science say that while the brain triggers action by sending powerful signals through the neuro system, just prior to those signals, the brain receives a signal from another part of the body. Weird as it may seem, according to some, that part is around your heart, the organ. Those who think this way say they have discovered that there is a group of cells that are identical to those in your brain; out of the heart area, a signal sparks and triggers the brain, and since the brain is where those subconscious programs run everything, the brain signal goes out to the other members of the body. Accordingly, they say, this heart signal does not activate all the time; it only participates in the activity of the body when it detects things on a deeper level and otherwise allows the subconscious to operate its programs without interference. According to this belief, this portion of the heart reacts and dictates to the subconscious programs when things are deep such as repeated hurt, traumatic, or moving experiences that imprint on the heart. Reactions from the heart can cause instant happiness or breakdown, sobbing, and remorse.

Biological science does not support the idea that there are brain cells in the heart. No cells around the heart match the cells in the brain. In addition, the communication between body parts and the brain is transmitted through neurons, not cells. This does not, however, negate the belief; it simply means this is not the way the heart runs the show. On the other hand, perhaps our understanding of the word heart in literature is too limited and takes in only the organ we know that pumps blood through the body. Just because science hasn't figured it out does not mean it is not true.

Think about this: until Einstein came along, Newtonian physics was absolutely the rule. Then in the early 1900s, with the publication of a few papers, quantum physics was born, and Newton's laws could not explain what was being observed and proven. You see, in the quantum realm, things do not behave like they should according to Newton.

In this same way, our understanding of the heart and what is meant by the word may or may not be accurate. Chances are, writings, such as those found in the Bible, are correct, and science simply hasn't matured to the point of understanding.

Some believe that the heart, not the organ, rather meaning the core of our being, sets parameters or rules of operation; some go so far as to say conviction dwells in the heart. If it is our core, this is where our values would reside, call it what you will; for simplicity, I call it the heart.

When a person believes, they will tend to fight for those beliefs; however, a person will die rather than betray their convictions unless, of course, a more powerful influence changes the heart or core and establishes a new conviction. Because of this, many believe it takes a very powerful source to etch a conviction in the heart. Wherever that core is, it seems to be the place where values or convictions dwell. As I said, for the sake of explaining, I will call it the heart. Although it might be referred to by some as conscience, in any case, it is the center of who we are. What we are in that place, which I now refer to as the heart, is what we really are.

The things in the heart are, for the most part, hidden from the subconscious and the conscious. Very few of us look deep enough into these things; we do not let our guard down long enough to examine the heart or what is going on in our lives because of the heart. Seldom, even when we examine our hearts, do we understand what we see. Without illumination from someone or something who does know our heart or how it impacts us, it leaves us knowing a mystery rather than a secret. The bottom line is we do not know our own hearts. I don't want to get preachy; however, the Bible tells us this. Sadly, most of us tend to look at that old book like we do an elderly person who we think is suffering from dementia; we listen, but then we think we know more or better.

An interesting note about the illumination of the heart. Consider some of the inventions created over the years; most who have created these things will describe how and when their "ah-ha" moment came. Extreme pressure, an inability to go on, and frustration after doing everything they could to produce results typically open the conscious mind to one of these moments—or perhaps it is better to say "prepares"—the conscious to receive one of these moments. I will talk more about this in a later chapter.

Speaking of the Bible, it is a key that provides a great deal of understanding about the heart and what takes place there. First Corinthians 13:5c (NIV) says that love "keeps no record of wrong." Few people realize the importance or impact of this statement when it comes to mankind. It appears, within the heart, there dwells an *inherited influence*, while holy love bares no record of wrong, which that opposite influence does. In fact, this influence we inherited keeps a record of every offense, no matter how small, and sooner or later, it will pull that offense out of the mothballs, throw it up on the conscious monitor of our life, and run the subconscious program that was filed away for the special occasion. Before we know it, we have done something that leaves us wondering why we did it. Romans

7:13–20 gives a very good description of this inner influence and conflict. I can't tell you how many times I asked the question, "Why?" Why did I do that? Why did I say that? Why did I react that way? My bad reactions seemed to fall on those closest to me, those considered my "loved ones."

Let me continue with some of the stories, and I think you will begin to see my point.

Ray describes the cause of being a broken believer as follows:

"My parents fought a lot; they had a very rocky relationship. When I was ten, one of my relatives told me my dad wasn't my dad. I confronted my mom about this, and she confirmed my biological father ran off, left her stranded, and she nearly starved to death. My grandparents rescued her and took care of her. After I was born, she met my stepfather, and they were married before my first birthday. They never spoke of the situation surrounding my birth and my mother's 'illegitimate child.' The turmoil within our family increased, causing so much stress. When I learned about my origins, I was heading into puberty, which is difficult enough. Now, at ten, I found I was not who I thought I was. Who was I? After all those years of thinking myself to be someone I wasn't, I was lost, angry,

*hurt, and broken beyond belief. I didn't believe, and I didn't believe people, creeds, rules—just about everything was beyond me. I took on a very deep feeling that everything in life was my fault. Everything was out of control. As a result, I developed an extremely controlling attitude; if things got disorganized, I freaked out. I would go on a rampage of violent rage. When it subsided, I felt terrible, and those around me were frightened of me as well. It was like I was possessed. When I was told to believe because the Bible or some expert said so, my subconscious program said, 'If your parents lied, what makes you think this is true? Don't trust anyone.' As a result, **I simply could not believe.**"*

Cathy

"I grew up without my father. My father abandoned me and my sister when I was five and my sister was three. My mother was a heroin addict; we grew up with abusive men in and out of my mother's life. My sister and I were dragged by my mother to crack houses so she could get high. There were no adults I could trust, and life was hard. At some point, my ability to believe was broken."

These stories might leave you thinking that this inner influence impacts only those with tragic childhoods and might lead you to the conclusion that tragic or dysfunctional family life is the real cause of the problem. However, there are many I have spoken to whose lives are not filled with tragedy. As an example, one of my friend's parents was a loving, hardworking, church-going parent; they were kind and full of wisdom. Here is Sandra's story.

Sandra

"Something inside of me told me I did not deserve to be a part of such a 'good' family. As a result, I fell into a very tragic lifestyle, a style which, if it had continued, would have ended my life before I was twenty-five. Something about the entire situation left me doubting my parents' love for me. When I lost that confidence in my parent's love, I lost my ability to believe."

Another friend, Fred, said this:

"My parents always taught me to be truthful; I went to church; when the minister asked me if I believed, I thought about it, and to be honest, I did not, so I said no. Instantly I became an outcast in that church. When I was old enough, I left that organization and found another that seemed to be one I would like to be a part of.

My Believer Is Broken

One day the minister asked me if I believed. Since nothing had changed in my heart, I told him no. The result was the same: I became an outcast. This happened a third time; only in this group, they tried to convince me by quoting Bible verses, asking questions, and making recommendations that they thought would convince me of the truth they were trying to promote. It didn't work, and after a time, they decided that I could not be helped and began pushing me away. I left that group broken and wishing I could believe and not knowing why I couldn't, but I was not going to lie about it just to be a part of that group."

You see, brokenness is not only for those whose life has broken through events. In the case of these friends, what seemed to be a healthy environment caused even greater issues. You will find children who grow up in what some would call a healthy environment, and that environment is just as toxic as those from brokenness. It may very well be the result of that inner influence. I challenge you to reflect on your own life, no matter what environment you grew up in, and see if this is not the case.

Again, these stories are not unique; they happen over and over throughout the world. It appears this inner influence takes every opportunity to ruin us. A friend of mine worked in a shop that made hip pins used in surgical hip replacements. He told me that when the inspector checks parts for flaws, they put the parts under a light that exposes even the smallest cracks or folds. If these parts are allowed to go out and are implanted in a person's hip, before long, the pin will fail. I see us, as humans, having several folds or cracks in our inner being. That inner influence seems to seek out those flaws and exploit them until they fester up and turn into full-blown infections that impact our lives. Someone once told me that if you took a newborn and put them in a perfect environment, after a period, something would rise to the surface in that child that would ruin the perfect environment.

What has all this got to do with me? The hurt handed down and the messages received from others, albeit some well intended on their part, because of offense harbored within my heart, ran certain programs that left me broken in the belief department. I have come to realize that a force (not human nature, more on this later) or influence inside of each of us has only one purpose: our destruction and keeping us from discovering our true potential (more on this later also). As a result of all that happened to me, which was not my fault, this inner influence used to break me down and isolate me from others, especially those who loved me. Seldom, if ever, did I recognize what was happening; because of this inner influence, I thought I was a horrible person; rather than disappoint myself or others, it was my horrible person image that began to live out in my life.

Only after a great deal of thought and illumination

from an outside force was I able to discover the root of all this. Believe it or not, my inner self-constructed image of myself being a bad person all began to emerge after one specific incident when I was growing up. Now, before you go off thinking, *Oh, yeah, this is just another one of those people who blame their parents for all their problems!* let me explain. Remember that inner influence? That inner thing will take advantage of every opportunity afforded it to destroy us by convincing us to identify with the person it is trying to convince us we are. In my case, that inner influence took a certain situation and convinced me it was my fault that it happened. After all, everyone was happy before I came into the picture; at least, that was the story that inner influence kept telling me. Was this the truth? Absolutely not; that did not alter the lie my inner influence had convinced me was true.

You might like to think you are exempt from this type of problem, the type of problem playing out in my life. That is not surprising, especially if you have not faced your own demons. I am not trying to convince you of anything; I am simply explaining how I arrived at a point of unbelief and that I was broken to the point I could not believe, no matter what I tried to do.

I want to add here that I have since spoken to several of my friends, who come from various situations—from horrible to near perfect—and many of them arrived at the same understanding and problem. They, like me, had a broken believer.

The influence these things have on a person's life can leave a great deal of brokenness. In my own life, when I felt out of control, I would react. In my situation, the program that kept running was "Hurt them, get away before they hurt and leave you." Because this was a program that ran without my conscious knowledge, what the slow-processing conscious me saw was not me doing something but rather others doing things to me.

Despite this, something inside of me kept looking and wanting to believe, drawing me on and hoping against all hope that someone or something would eventually be able to convince me or enable me to believe. Believe in anything or anyone. I kept thinking, *Am I the only one?*

There is a story in the Bible about a man named Thomas. He was told by all his friends that Jesus was alive; he was told this three days after Thomas had seen Jesus' dead body and knew that Jesus had been crucified. Thomas said, "Unless I see the nail marks in his hands and put my finger where the nails were, and put my hand into his side, I will not believe" (John 5:25). This pretty much described me. It didn't matter what people told me; I needed proof, or I would not believe. No, it was more than that; *I could not believe.*

If you think about a person who has had a stroke and can't use their hand or a leg as a result—that was me; that portion of a person that allows them to believe a thing was, in me, incapable of believing. I needed healing. The proof required to enable me to believe had to be a lot of proof, undeniable proof. This set up an incredible inner drive to know the truth, and I developed an ability to sift through all manner of information and quickly discover flaws in things.

Sadly, this ability to find flaws included people, and that further isolated me. I would meet someone, and without realizing it, I began to evaluate them, not looking for the good things about them but their flaws. When I discovered them, I would expose the flaw, usually in public, much to the person's embarrassment. The result was always the same: I would be alone again.

From my weakness came strength. I was able to quickly eliminate false information and dig until I found the truth. I think that is what led me to pursue a career in archeology. I liked working with artifacts, sorting out information, tossing aside the false, and digging down until I discovered the truth. When I started my career, I never dreamed it would lead me to a project called the Migdal Project, but that is another story. As I said earlier, my career led me to Chicago and to a series of events that would change my life forever.

One last reminder before I leave this subject. This inner influence is not isolated to a limited group of people, such as those coming from divorce, abuse, or abandonment situations that leave them with foster, step, or adoptive-parent childhoods. It seems all of us struggle with that inner influence no matter what our lives are like.

It also appears that inner influence does not stop with childhood. We, as adults, continue to be held down and even destroyed by that inner thing. I firmly believe it hinders us all the time in no other way than telling us we are not, or cannot be, what we were born to do and be. Based on what I have experienced, I believe each of us can overcome this inner influence to some extent, and most do in certain things, but it is always messing with our minds. It is a struggle that prevents us from reaching our true potential, no matter how high we rise. It shows up in our lives in some of the strangest ways, either by overindulgence in our strengths or overindulgence in our weaknesses.

I want to share a couple more cases with you that were uncovered from discussions with people, events that took place later in their lives, and events that caused a broken believer.

The first comes from an older man in his seventies. I share this not to judge but rather to set the stage for the story of my quest. Bob seemed to be living a comfortable life in retirement. One day he was talking with me, telling me some of his personal story.

Bob

"My wife Beatrice is suffering from Alzheimer's in the last stages, and she is in a nursing home.

I have been a dutiful husband visiting her daily, feeding her, and staying with her; she seems to know me. She has been tearful much of the time at her inability to function, but deeper than that, she carries a lot of sadness over events in her life. We both carry a load of guilt, dragging it around like a bag full of heavy stones. Each day seems to add weight to the bag we carry. The weight of that bag is exceedingly heavy, to the point I can't carry it any longer.

"When we were younger, Beatrice had been unfaithful to our marriage and had gotten pregnant by another man. When I found out about the infidelity, I was broken, yet despite her bad choices, I was willing to forgive her, and we decided to do our best to mend our broken relationship. However, allowing the child to be born was never going to be a part of our life, and we decided to abort the baby. Later in life, at a time when we were ready to move into another phase of our life, Beatrice became pregnant again; this time, the child was mine. However, the inconvenience of a child this late in life was not in our plans, so we aborted this child as well.

"I feel my wife's disease is the result of God punishing us. I've been to various religious leaders, and they did their best to convince me

> *that God forgives us, but I just cannot believe it. As a result, the burden of this continues. I feel what we have done is so horrible there was no way God would forgive us. I just cannot believe."*

I am not sharing this story to point judgment at anyone; I am simply telling you about how one individual, not a child, arrived at a point of being unable to believe. For some of us, the things we choose, the abuses we dole out, and the brokenness we promote are so great, and our guilt over them so strong, no matter what another person says, we cannot find it within ourselves to lay the burden of it down. I would venture to say every one of us finds ourselves, at some point, examining something we are extremely sorrowful for; many of us find it impossible to believe we can be or are forgiven. The result is a broken believer.

Parents can sometimes cause issues by thinking and having to live with the idea of "tough love." Kyle had gone astray, and his life was an embarrassment to his parents. As a result, they cut him off and told him until he "straightened up" not to return. They didn't want him around if he was going to "act like that." They pushed him away and disowned him. Their hope was that he would wake up. They thought he was the prodigal son and were convinced their son would wake up; however, that is not the way the Prodigal Son story played out; in that story, the son chose to leave, but his father did not cast him out, because of the son's unruly ways. The truth they faced was something quite different. Many times, our mouth says what we want to hear, not what our heart is saying. Many times, with a child who continues to act up, parents just get tired of dealing with them and want them to go away. There are situations that lead to this type of feeling, a feeling that perhaps that person just isn't worth all the trouble. The message Kyle heard from his parents was not one of "wake up" but simply to "get out; we don't love you enough to put up with you."

As a result, Kyle, instead of waking up, went to sleep one night with a handful of pills and a bottle of whiskey and never woke up again. His parents were devastated, they wanted so much to hold their son in their arms and beg him to come home just like he was, but in this case, it was too late.

Steve and Carrol carried a burden that none of the religious tricks could remove. They simply had no power to believe they were forgiven by their son, and he was gone, his voice was silenced. I heard a very wise man say, "If you discipline a child, you must follow it up with love." Extending love to their child was not going to happen. As a result, they had a broken believer.

One last case. Dennis started drinking alcohol when he was thirteen. As he grew older, he married and had children. He provided his wife and children with very little; he drank away businesses and their money to the point they barely had enough to live on. Dennis tried multiple times to stop drinking, but he felt like he could not. To add to the reduction in family finance, Dennis was a smoker, and some of what was left over after drinking went up in smoke in the form of cigarettes. Dennis felt horrible, he wanted to stop, tried to stop, and sought out help to stop, but nothing worked. Dennis knew he was an alcoholic, and there wasn't anything anyone could do to help.

Dennis sought out several clergymen over the years, hoping they would have the answer. Many of them offered "salvation" to him if he would only believe. By this point in Dennis's life, he had failed so many times and carried such guilt over what he had done to his wife and children he could not believe that God would forgive him. When a minister would tell him he was forgiven, he didn't believe it. When the minister shared scripture and said things like, "You do believe the Bible, don't you?" Dennis was so broken that none of the religious tricks worked. Some would say, "Dennis, confess your sins and ask God to forgive you." He would, and after that, the minister would say, "God's word says if we confess our sins, God is faithful and just to forgive us. Do you believe?" At that point, Dennis would turn and sadly walk away, saying, "No, I don't!" His burden was not lifted; he trudged on with his heavy bag of stones. On each of the stones was written a different time he tried and failed.

My point in all of this is to help you understand that, for many of us, believing because of books collected over centuries, regardless of where they originated, falls silent at the feet of those with a broken believer. Those written words do not have the power to bring life; they bring only death and disappointment. As much as we would like them to produce the power to believe, they do not.

For Bob, Dennis, Steve, Carrol, the friends whose stories I have shared, and me, telling us to believe is like telling a person with no right hand to use it. Inside of many, maybe most, perhaps all of us, the ability to really believe without a far deeper proof, far deeper than the written word or those spoken by humans, is required. Our believer is broken or dead, and we have no power to resurrect it.

This is the condition I was in when something changed all of that. As hard as I tried, I could not believe because my believer was broken.

CHAPTER 2

THE STRAW THAT BROKE THE CAMEL'S BACK

My great-grandmother used a phrase that meant it was the last thing laid on me that was too much for me to carry. When she would erupt in anger, she would say, "That was the straw that broke the camel's back." I reached that point one night.

It was late summer when I started to attend religious meetings with a small group of people who seemed to be genuine and poised to make discoveries that would change the world. The group leaders were a nice young couple. Danny was a financial planner working for a prestige financial institution in downtown Chicago. Amanda, his wife, was a real estate agent who primarily sold downtown condominiums to upward-mobile young professionals. That is how I met them. I was in the market for a place, and a friend gave me Amanda's business card. I liked Amanda from the start. She wasn't the pushy type; she was more laid back, listening to me and taking a lot of interest in the ideas I had for a condo.

I purchased my current condo from her. After the sale, our relationship continued, and I joined the group she and Danny were leading. The group met weekly and discussed religious topics. As usual, it went well for me in the group, then that inner program thing began to work its magic. Our group was discussing what each of us had dealt with in our lives and how it was impacting us. Each person in the group told how they came to a place in their lives when they decided to believe in a particular thing that gave not only meaning but clarity to them. Each of them said they simply decided to believe based on reading a certain proclamation of beliefs. It was at that point I realized that these people were all part of the same religious organization.

I grew up attending various churches from time to time; from those churches, I gathered enough information to understand that each of the organizations had some type of creed or core beliefs. The process went something like this: you listen to their creed, you make your decision, then you simply believe. I suspect it was a decision to *follow the rules* of that organization more than *believing* those rules.

I have discovered with most, if not all, of these groups, failure to either comply or to simply question those creeds or statements of beliefs can get you into trouble, especially if you prove them wrong, or at least prove they are not completely accurate. Joining those groups is more like joining a club; I've always thought a church should be more like a group filled with love, compassion, forgiveness, and understanding, not demanding.

As I stated before, belief, or better stated, submission, doesn't happen in my life like that. People think I'm a non-believer because of my unwillingness to accept what is being said, even when people are my friends, and they all believe a thing. The truth is I am an unable-to-believer; there is a world of difference between the two. What it takes some to believe doesn't work with me; I need proof, undeniable, concrete proof. It is how I flow; as I have already explained, in my past, those closest to me were willing to either lie or withhold information from me. Why would I trust people who were not as close to me when I couldn't trust those closest to me? That was the program running in my inmost being; as a result, I built a wall—no, it was bigger than a wall; it was a complete fortress with huge guns protecting it. No one could get in; it was my safe place, a very lonely safe place.

Not only is this true of me, but once convinced, I am all in! Sadly, others do not seem to live within that type of honesty. Churches are filled with people who, because of their desire to be accepted by a group or the group they are associated with, say they believe when in all honesty, they simply submit to a system that supports whatever belief they are buying into. When you get away from the "Church," the life they live is contradictory to the life they portray when with the "Church people." At one time, I described them as "hypocrites," but I have come to realize they are not really hypocrites. My understanding of them now, after my quest, I have realized there is a powerlessness in their lives that stems from a lack of conviction-based belief. They have settled for what was offered, not knowing that there is something better out there.

In my desire to believe, when I attach myself to a thing, I will follow it completely until such a time that it proves untrue or flawed. As I mentioned earlier, this is one of my strengths. I don't have to spend a lot of time and effort on this; many times, a quick mental experiment settles the issue for me.

The group I was involved in, once they found out my difficulty with belief, kept offering various ways or tricks to get me to make a commitment to their belief. At first, because I really liked all these people, I tried very hard to follow their suggestions. However, after a period that lasted several weekly meetings, they were getting irritated with me and my lack of willingness to give in. I, on the other hand, was very frustrated with their inability to offer me something that could help me; there was growing tension over the entire matter. Finally, attempting to get me to make my *decision*, Danny said, "Why are you even coming here if you don't want to get on board with our beliefs?"

I'm sure, now, he didn't mean it the way it either

sounded or the way I took it, but at that moment, I felt he was giving me an ultimatum: "Either get on board or get out." I was hurt. I felt more broken than I have ever felt. All the disappointments and ruined relationships in my life came crashing in on me in that one moment, and my heart and hope broke. Remember what I said about the heart? It pulls out of mothballs past hurtful events and then uses them against us. Well, there it was; every offense handed out by a religious group that ever passed through my life rose to the surface of my conscious mind.

I had endured many meetings of this type over the years, meetings in which well-meaning people were trying to give me advice that would help me believe. Most of these people were suggesting the things that got them to give in and finally accept what was being told to them by other people. If you are not familiar with those tactics, they usually follow a certain pattern. Many start out with, "It is in the Bible; you do believe the Bible, don't you?" I hate fighting with people; however, I also will not be bullied into saying I believe a thing I really don't believe. When you use a statement like the one I have just shared, my response is not "Yes, I do" My flight or fight mechanism kicks in, and I erupt, or I run.

I'm always amazed by people who utilize the "You do believe the Bible, don't you?" question; it is as if they think everybody believes the Bible. Here is my take on the Bible; it is a historical book filled with words that either God or man stated in the past that have been altered to fit and reach the society that surrounds it. If you want to understand what it is saying, you must look at several translations and understand the culture the translation was attempting to reach. You also must take into consideration the period in history in which it was either written or translated. For example, when a letter written by the Apostle Paul speaks of scripture, his letter is not the scripture he is talking about. To him, a Jew and a former Pharisee, chances are very good that he was referring to the Torah; his own writings were merely letters, not Scripture. However, today, many people consider his letters part of Scripture, which in his day and in his culture, they were not.

I hope you can see why the group's suggestions were, to me, so aggravating. To me, they were all tricks to get me to give up and accept. One of the members in the group suggested praying out loud, as if that had some magical ability to produce belief. I'm sure, in their experience, it was the thing that convinced them that they were indeed committed, or at that moment, they committed to that organization's belief.

I recall another person telling me that if I read the New Testament from Matthew to Revelation, by the time I was done, I would believe. I did read, and it did not result in belief.

Each time someone suggested I do something, I genuinely tried what they suggested because I really wanted to believe, but the power to believe just wasn't in me. I, like

The Straw That Broke the Camel's Back

Thomas of old, needed to stick my fingers in the holes. Nothing short of that seemed to be able to convince me.

The pressure to believe was on, and I could not—not that I would not, I could not. I was broken and felt I was strange and different from all of them. I simply could not believe; the ability to do so was not in me. I could have lied and stayed with the group, saying, "Oh, now I see. Okay, now I believe," but that would have been a lie, and I am not a liar. At that moment, I sensed my fight instinct kicking in, and I was ready to unload on these people, just like I had done so many times in the past, but I hesitated. I really liked this group, and, after all, they were only trying to help me in my unbelief; they simply did not know how to help me. What I realized at that moment was that they could not; they did not have the answers or the power to enable me to believe.

As a result, I grabbed my coat, and I ran away into the night, hurting and broken, wondering what was wrong with me. Was there any hope for me, or was I doomed to unbelief and loneliness for the rest of my life? Why did I have to be so weird? Why couldn't I be normal like everyone else I met? Things were so hard for me to accept. Why? Was there no hope for me?

I ran several blocks through the streets of Chicago toward my condo before I slowed to a walk. My heart was breaking, and my lungs were ripping at the walls of my chest. All those years, all those relationships, all my brokenness kept welling up from my heart, and I wept bitterly. Was there no one who could rescue me from this ongoing struggle?

I was only a few blocks from my condo when I walked past it: a small store with a display window dimly lit. The only businesses that were open that late at night were the bars, clubs, and restaurants, yet there was a little shop in the middle of them. It was out of place; it didn't belong in the location it was in. I peered into the display window.

As I looked at the items in the display window, they all appeared broken, a wheel missing here, a partial nameplate, an outside doorway with no door, a doll with one arm missing, and a book with no cover. *What kind of junk store is this?* I thought to myself as I gazed at the items. I glanced to the left of the window, and there was the sign stating "*open*" that struck me as odd for a shop to be open at this time of night. Curiosity got the best of me; I dried my eyes, opened the door, and went in.

CHAPTER 3
Lost, Not Broken

Have you ever decided on a thing that, at the time, seemed so simple that you barely recognized it as a decision, and before you knew it, your life was completely changed? That was how my decision to step into that store was. Everything about that store was strange; the lighting was dim, the merchandise was broken, and some of it appeared new and some very old.

It wasn't an antique store. It really looked more like a hoarder's home, with stuff stacked up all over and shelves filled with odd items that did not fit together. What I mean is that there was no flow to it. You would, for example, expect coats to be positioned with other coats, toys with toys, and housewares with housewares, but this place was a mess. There was one odd shoe on a shelf next to a teacup with the handle missing, a toy steam engine missing one push rod, and a pair of glasses with one of the lenses missing. As I looked over the items, each flaw seemed to glow. I already explained my ability to see the flaws in people, and the glow merely provided me with an assist in discovering the flaws in the items. I thought to myself, *Why would anyone display this junk? Did they seriously expect someone to buy it? This is high-rent State Street in Chicago. How does this place stay open?*

I felt alone in the store, with no other customers, and where was the salesperson? I spent a few minutes browsing through the items, taking note of the missing parts when my eyes suddenly landed on a shield and a sword hanging on a display rack. I walked over to the display rack and took note that they both appeared to be from the Roman Empire era. As I looked, they did not appear to be fake. These were not the first artifacts I had seen of this nature; however, their condition was so new they looked like they had just been made. With one exception: they had battle marks on them.

The shield appeared to have been struck many times by a weapon, the shield successfully fending off the attacks. This was extremely interesting to me; after all, what were the chances of finding something of this nature in a junk shop? The workmanship of the shield was remarkable, and it was decorated, which meant it was the possession of a seasoned warrior who had faced many battles, probably a dignitary or an officer.

This shield was the discovery of a lifetime for a person in my profession; careers are made with items like this.

First, you dig down to discover the history and how it arrived at the point you discovered it. Then you try to find out who it originally belonged to, the battles it was used in, and things like that. Once you have its history, you write and submit papers about your findings, and they are published in professional trade journals. Then you start giving lectures. This seemed too good to be true. As I looked at it, I could see a part of the shield was missing. For a moment, I felt sad because if it had been completely intact, it would be more valuable; however, even in its current condition, it was worth more than everything else in the store—priceless is the word I would use.

Then there was the sword. The craftsmanship of this item was glaring; the detail and quality were such as I had never seen. At first, I thought it was a fake, a copy; but as I looked closer, I could tell it was very old, and it, too, was used. After you have examined several items like this over the years, you develop an eye for antiquity. This was not a modern replica, this was the real deal, or at least it appeared to be. I needed to examine it more closely. As I moved in a little closer, I could see that something was missing from the sword as well. My heart sank; why was everything in this store broken?

The Capulus of the sword, or the hilt—that's the part that runs from the blade to the end of the handle—was decorated, which told me it belonged to a dignitary or an officer. The Obviabis, or weight on the end that gave balance to the sword and prevented the holder's hand from slipping off the end of the handle, was missing.

The Pelpate, or handle, had writing on it. I couldn't make out what the letters were, but they appeared to be Greek, not Latin. Latin would make sense, given the period it was created in, had it been a common soldier who wielded it. However, Greek was the common language of the elites at the time this sword might have been produced. Given the decorations on it, the Greek letters added to my suspicions about the original owner and their status or position in the army. Everything about this sword told me it and the shield might be a matching set, which would be a real treasure, a treasure a person might sell everything they had to purchase, a real pearl of great price, so to speak.

Curiosity got the best of me; I reached out and took hold of the shield, and lifted it from its position on the display rack.

Suddenly everything changed. My surroundings turned from a junk store to a wide-open battlefield, with soldiers all around me, daylight instead of darkness. This was no longer Chicago; I was standing in the territory of the Roman Empire. My surroundings were not of the current age, and this was not a recreation of a battle from antiquity; this was the real thing. I could hear the moans from those who had been wounded; I could smell the smells of battle, the stench of sweat and blood mingled. I nearly vomited.

Choking back my nausea, I looked around; there were

thousands of soldiers all over the battlefield. Many of them were being cut down by an enemy that appeared more like a mist than flesh and blood. Where was I, and who was this enemy?

Then I noticed something; there were, amid this army of soldiers, several people, both men and women, who were successfully fighting the mist enemy. I looked closer, and each of them had a shield and sword nearly identical to the one I was holding in my hand. Their shield, however, was not broken but complete; nothing was missing. They all had different attire, not the typical Roman soldier attire of that period. Some of the people looked like they had stopped by this battle after working in an office building in the city; others appeared to be from various centuries from B.C. through current A.D. How confusing! Then I saw something else, each of the people who held a shield like mine had crowns on their heads, giving me the understanding they were the elite, but why were people of such standing fighting in a battle in the Roman Empire around 100 A.D.?

As I turned to my right, there was a woman soldier, strong and solid. You could tell she had faced many battles, yet there was a freshness about her; she was wearing Roman battle gear, and yet she appeared as if she were at a ball having the time of her life. On my left was a young man holding a sword that was gleaming like the sun. It was sharper than any sword I had ever seen. He was strong and powerful, ready to fight, and experienced with the sword like nothing I had ever seen. This guy was incredible, striking down the enemy like they were nothing.

Suddenly I felt a jolt. I turned, and there in front of me was a frightening-looking mist warrior. He/She had just struck my shield with their drawn sword, and they were ready to strike again. I say "he/she" because the enemy warrior was neither man nor woman but something else, like both and neither. After the first blow, I knew I couldn't take another, I was wounded, and I could feel myself slipping. Another blow would leave me unconscious. Weakened by the first strike, I felt the shield slip from my hand and hit the ground. There I stood defenseless; this was the end; I was going to die. I felt myself dropping to the ground when suddenly, the woman on my right grabbed my arm and held me up, using her shield to protect me from the impending blow from the enemy.

Then, as if it never happened, my surroundings changed back to the junk store. Someone was holding my arm to steady me. I looked to my right, and there was an old woman wearing what seemed to be a peasant's attire. I regained my composure and stepped back in astonishment. What in the world had just happened to me, and who was this old woman?

"Are you okay, my dear?" I could hear her saying the words; however, I was unable to speak. With that, she tugged on my arm and sat me down in a chair close to the display where the shield hung as if it had never been touched; with one exception, the sword was now gone.

I sat there confused and having trouble focusing. My eyes were still swollen from my emotional ordeal prior to entering the store. What had just happened? After a minute or two, I was finally able to speak, and the first words out of my mouth were, "What just happened?"

In response, the old woman said, "I'm not sure, my dear, you nearly fainted as if struck by something, and I grabbed your arm to steady you. Are you alright?"

Her words seemed to come from a much younger woman, a woman like the one that had just protected me. I shook my head and said, "No, I'm not alright. What just happened? The last thing I remember was grabbing that shield and sword on the rack, and suddenly everything changed."

The old woman looked puzzled and said, "What sword? There is only the shield hanging there. You saw a sword too?"

"Of course, there was a sword! It must be lying on the floor; I probably dropped it." As I said the words, I looked around and couldn't find it. How could something that big disappear? It had to be there. I was holding it in my hand. Or was I? When I stopped and thought about it, I realized I had never removed it from the leather binding that attached it to my back. The sword was gone.

"Very peculiar!" the old woman said. "Brea, my name is Kayla. I help here at the store. The sword you speak of has been missing for a very long time, and until now, no one else has seen it; you are the first in many years."

"Nice to meet you, Kayla," I said, a little puzzled by the sudden disappearance of the sword. Then it hit me, "How do you know my name? We just met!" I nearly shouted. Fear started welling up inside, and my fight or flight was kicking into overdrive. Then she touched my hand, and suddenly calm came over me. I felt like I had known this woman all my life. For some strange reason, I felt no fear, only peace. I settled back in the chair as a child would do, waiting for Grandma to hand her a freshly baked cookie and a glass of milk.

Kayla smiled and said, "Wait here. I have something in the back for you that I believe has been waiting for you to show up." With that, she disappeared. I could hear her rummaging around in the back as if she were sorting through things, looking for a thing that had been shuffled around so much that it was now hard to find. Suddenly, she appeared back at my side. No, I don't mean she walked back; I mean she suddenly appeared as if she had never walked away. In her hand was a small leather pouch with letters on it. I stared at the pouch in disbelief; my name was on the pouch, "Brea Rea Joyce"!

Fear started to swell up, and I could feel it in the pit of my stomach again; I was ready to bolt when Kayla spoke,

"I believe this is yours."

I was astonished and blurted out, "What kind of junk store is this, and why is my name on that pouch?"

With that, Kayla started to explain, "Nothing in the store is junk, they are items with parts missing, and they are here waiting for their owners to show up. The items claim the owner, and the owner helps the items find their missing parts. The items are here, and the owners are lost!" She continued, "This pouch has been here since you were... Well, a very long time."

I looked at her in disbelief, which should not surprise anyone. After all, how could anyone expect me, a person who can't believe, to believe something this weird? Kayla held out the pouch for me to take. I sat there, unable to move. Something inside of me was afraid to take it. An "awkward moment" would not begin to describe that moment.

"I'm curious about the sword," Kayla said as she changed the direction of the conversation. I think she realized I was not ready to take the leather pouch, so she continued, "Tell me about the sword. What did it look like, and what was missing?" With those words, she once again offered me the pouch.

This time I reached out and took hold of the pouch. Suddenly the entire place was full of light, and I could see things like never before. It startled me, and I turned loose of the pouch, but it clung to me as if it were my skin. I jumped up from my chair and said, "I don't have time for all this nonsense. I have no idea why I am even in here!" With that, I threw the pouch in her direction high above her head; with the reflexes of a professional ball player, Kayla grabbed the pouch. I was astonished by the swift movement of this old woman; her body never moved, yet without looking, she raised her hand and caught the pouch. With that, I bolted out the door and shouted, "This is insane. I am out of here!" I ran the last few blocks to my condo, looking back as I ran to make sure no one was following me.

I punched in the code to my condo's front door, opened the door, stepped inside, slammed the door behind me, and locked every lock I was able to lock. I checked it again; dead bolt on, chain lock on, then I set the alarm system. I had no idea what had just happened, but I wanted to make sure nothing was going to get in and harm me.

I got ready for bed, and my head was spinning. Reflections of the group meeting boiled up in my head. I realized it happened again; I broke away from a group I really wanted to be a part of. Why couldn't they give me the answers? Why couldn't they help me? Why did I have to be so odd, different from everyone else? Other people in these groups seemed to have no problem believing. What was it they had that I didn't? I sat on the floor of the shower, water pouring over me and tears flowing from me. "Why can't I believe? Is there no one who can help me?" I'm not sure how long I sat there; it seemed like an hour.

Then as suddenly as the tears had erupted, they stopped, and my mind flashed back to the store and its items with missing parts. What did Kayla mean by "the owners were lost"? What was that pouch Kayla tried to give me? Why was my name on it? Although I was alone, I spoke out loud and said, "I don't recall ever owning a pouch like that! It felt heavier than it should have when I held it; the thing felt like it had an entire lifetime of collectibles in it. What was that light all about?"

It was late, and I was worn out from the emotional and physical stress I had just put myself through. I readied myself for bed, and sure I would fall asleep as soon as my head hit the pillow. I was not wrong; I barely remember pulling the covers over me, I had one last thought about Kayla and that battle scene, and I was out. Sound asleep, peaceful, restful sleep until 3 a.m. Suddenly, a voice—the voice of someone in my bedroom—woke me from my sound sleep.

The voice sounded close yet far away, like an echo. I sat straight up in bed and looked around, fully expecting to see someone standing over me; my fists were clenched, and I was ready to strike out at whoever was in my room. I looked, and the room was empty; the slow tick of my antique alarm clock was the only sound in the room. I got up, went to the doors and windows, and checked them to make sure no one had broken in. One last check of the alarm system told me everything was locked up, so what was the voice? I shook my head and said, "Get a grip, Brea. You had a rough night. Don't let the creepiness of the events at that store ruin the rest of your night's sleep."

With that, I settled back into my bed and started drifting off again. Suddenly that same voice spoke again, and this time I understood what it said. The voice was saying, "Brea, help me, come back, don't leave me here. I need you!" I sat straight up in my bed and said, "Who are you, who is there, what is it you want?" With that, the room went silent again. I tried to go to sleep; however, by that point, I was too stressed out to force more sleep. I laid there for a short period of time, or at least it seemed like it, and then it came again, the voice saying, "Brea, come back; don't leave me here. I need you to find the missing piece." I was horrified. How was this possible? I'm a practical person; this is crazy, yet my mouth opened, and I said out loud, "Where are you, and how can I help?" The voice replied, "You know where I am. You held me in the store. We need to finish the journey. Come back!"

This wasn't really happening. I was sure I was still asleep and having a weird dream, hearing voices with no one around. I've never seen a therapist, but this was scaring me. What was happening to me? I was sure I was losing it. Yet something inside, deep inside, responded to the call, and without using my mouth, words seemed to flow out from somewhere, and I said, "I will return in the morning!" With that, I fell fast asleep and didn't wake up until 8 a.m. It was Saturday, and I had no plans. I woke up, freshened up, got dressed, put on my makeup, and set out for the store.

I suddenly realized I wasn't even sure where it was. Then I remembered the restaurant that was next door. I knew exactly where it was, yet for the life of me, I didn't remember ever having seen the store before. I had walked up and down State Street many times; there were a couple of blocks where the sidewalk narrowed, and that was where the store was Friday night.

I hurried down the blocks leading up to where I believed the store was located. I walked past the restaurant that bordered the store, and the store wasn't there. I said to myself, "Settle down, Brea, don't panic. It was late, you were upset, and you probably have the wrong location." With that, I turned, walked two blocks down, rounded the corner, and still nothing, I slowly walked back past the restaurant where I was sure the store had been, but I saw nothing. The manager of the restaurant had just arrived; I described the store and asked him if he recalled where it might be. He laughed and said, "Young lady, you must have the wrong block. There has never been a store like that around here. I've been here for over twenty years, and nothing as you described has ever opened here." with that, he disappeared behind the door, and I heard it lock as he closed it. I got the message; he was pretty much ending any further questions about a nonexistent store.

I turned and started walking back to my condo when I heard the voice again, "Brea, don't leave; come back. Help me, please!" I turned around and started walking back toward the restaurant. The store had to be somewhere around that place. Just before I reached the restaurant, there was an alley on the side of the restaurant. I glanced to my left, then back to my right, and as I did, there it was: the store. For the first time, I saw the sign above the display window. It read "Second Chance."

Common sense would tell me not to go back in; something was wrong with this entire matter. Yet the voice sounded so familiar, and something inside me wanted to know what this was all about. I glanced at my phone; the time read 10 a.m. I reached out, grabbed the door handle, pressed my thumb on the release lever, pushed the door open, and went inside.

Like the night before, the store was void of people. It was just me and the junk—sorry, I mean items with missing owners. I quickly walked by the shelves piled high with "items." I had one specific item in mind, that shield. I didn't care about the rest of the store; I just needed to get to that shield. Two isles down and then to the left, and there it was, hanging right where I first saw it, but this time there was no sword. What happened to the sword? Kayla told me the sword had been missing for years, yet it was there last night, and now it was gone. I spoke up, "Hello! Kayla, are you here? Is anyone here?" Suddenly, there was a commotion in the next aisle. I stepped around to see what at first looked like the warrior woman who had saved me from that sword strike the night before. I blinked, and there before me was the old woman, Kayla. After what I had just gone through, this didn't surprise me; nothing seemed to be what appeared. In fact, things seemed to appear and disappear on me every time I blinked.

Kayla said, "Hello, Brea. I'm so glad you came back. Are you ready to take back the pouch? It has been here such a long time, and it seems to be getting heavier by the day. Are you ready to start your quest?"

"What quest?" I blurted out, "I need to talk to you because so many weird things are happening. I don't understand. I need some answers."

"What is wrong, my dear? You asked for help. You wanted to know what was wrong with you. That was your cry last night, wasn't it?"

I'm sure the look on my face was one of shock and horror; I was alone the night before, in the shower. How could she possibly know I cried out? Was it a prayer or simply a cry of desperation? No matter if she wasn't there, how did she know? How did she know my name? What was this place? I needed answers; things were out of control, and I don't like things out of control; I must control things! Panic was setting in, fight or flight. Which would it be?

CHAPTER 4
THE QUEST

"Please have a seat, Brea, and I will try to help you understand." The old woman, Kayla, reached out her hand to direct me to the chair that I had settled in the night before. As she stretched out her arm, I noticed a bracelet, not really a bracelet, an armband like those worn by ancient soldiers in battle to protect the forearm, another piece of armor from a bygone era. Kayla ignored my obvious question as she pulled up a chair next to me and sat down.

"First, let me tell you that you are not an unknown where I come from. We have been watching you for a very long time, preparing for this moment and your arrival at this very place. You like to be in control of everything, don't you? This is one thing you will have no control over if you decide to start this journey. This quest will take you to places, and you will see things you have never dreamed of. If you choose to take this journey, I will go with you every step of the way, you will never be alone, and I will not leave you. Do you believe me?"

Really? This is what all of this has come to? Am I supposed to believe someone I'm not even sure exists? Realistically, I'm sitting in what is probably an alley, not a store, just off State Street in downtown Chicago, looking like a fool who has lost her mind, talking to someone who isn't there. This is crazy; all of this is way out of range for me. I can't even control my mouth; at this point, it opens, and words come out without me trying to speak; in fact, I'm trying to keep my mouth shut, but my mouth won't listen to me, it opens, and the words come pouring out "I believe."

Why did I say that? In my head, I'm thinking, *Shut up!* but something deeper down is crying out, "I believe you." It continues to flow from somewhere deep down inside. In my head, I am saying, "I want to, I want it to be real, but how can it be? Everyone lets me down, nobody is there for me, I'm alone, I'm broken, I can't believe," yet the words that came out of my mouth were "I believe." Tears welled up in my eyes. I couldn't say anything more, I could only think thoughts, and I was terrified that this was just another disappointment.

Kayla's smile was warm and reassuring. She took her hand, put it on my shoulder, and gently squeezed it. Suddenly, I felt a connection I'd never experienced before. I felt like she was my twin, and with her at my side, I would never be alone again.

The Quest

With that, she said, "The leather pouch is of your own making. You placed the first items in it when you were very young, it was a heavy thing for a little girl to carry, but you held onto it. Take it up and take it with you; soon, you will know what to do with it. You poor child, it is such a heavy burden you carry. That, however, will soon change." Kayla's words broke into a very deep and dark place in my heart, a place I knew existed but was afraid to go.

She continued, "The shield you took hold of yesterday, it took you somewhere, didn't it? Tell me about it and tell me about the sword. I'm very curious why it appeared to you."

I began to explain what happened when I grabbed the shield, the battlefield, the young woman warrior who saved me, and the powerful young soldier next to us. He was dressed in Templar attire; at least, it appeared to be Templar attire. Without a closer look, I couldn't be sure. I told her about the various people on the battlefield with crowns and how they were successfully striking down the enemy, but then there were others who were being struck down and had no defense at all. "Kayla," I said, "Who were they, and why were they being killed? I had the shield, but it was no defense against the enemy. If it wasn't for the young woman warrior, I am sure I would have died right then and there. Was it real?"

"Most things are—whether they are or not—if they are real to you. Tell me about the sword and the man holding it," she responded.

"The sword was sharp, well-maintained, and it was decorated. Everything about it told me it was the possession of someone of great status. Something was missing, the weight at the end that gave it balance; without the weight, the sword was useless." I responded. The sword... I wondered why Kayla was so interested in the sword.

"Seldom has anyone ventured out on a quest with two items in their possession; the shield is yours, it is missing a piece, and the piece has a name on it. That name is important; it gives the shield power." she continued, "The sword, that one is curious. That should belong to someone else, and I believe you will need to help someone else find their lost piece as you seek to find your lost piece. Tell me about the young man who was with you on the battlefield."

"He was a warrior dressed in Templar attire. Now that I think about it, he had a sword but no shield. I'm not sure how he was protecting himself." I paused for a moment and then asked, "Who was the warrior woman who saved me?"

"You will need to discover that answer for yourself, Brea; often, the first experience with an item reveals what has not yet been seen to prepare you for a moment when all things will become clear. If you are ready, I need you to do one thing, and with that, you will be off on your quest. Are you ready?"

Of course I wasn't ready. I didn't know what this was

all about. I needed to do research; I needed to find out more about Kayla and discover her flaws so I could expose them; I needed to know more about the shield and the sword, and I needed to know more about the store. Why was it not there, and why did it suddenly appear? And how in the world did a shield speak to me? So many questions, and so much was out of control. No, I wasn't ready; I opened my mouth to tell her no, and when I did, "Yes, I am ready!" is what came out.

Why did I say that? I'm not ready; I have a million things to do to prepare, answers need to be listed, I need to evaluate them, and then decide if any of this is true. *No, I'm not ready*, I thought, but my mouth opened again, and it said, "What do you need me to do?" It seemed that something deep down inside of me had taken control of my mouth.

With that, Kayla said, "Walk over and take the shield off the rack, please." I did as she requested; I figured that if I did that, I could come back to her and start getting answers to all my questions. However, the moment I removed the shield from the rack and had it in my hands, the store disappeared, and I was standing, not on a battlefield, but based on what happened next, somewhere around the late 1700 or early 1800s. I was probably in the US. My surroundings made me think I was most likely on the East Coast, maybe Virginia, Maryland, or possibly New York; not sure why I thought that, but I was soon to find out I was correct.

This was not what I expected. On the other hand, I didn't know what to expect. Why here? That morning as I left my condo, I dressed in a wool skirt and wore knee-high boots, a sweater, and a leather vest. Currently, I was wearing something long and layered, not like a pilgrim, but not modern. It was a long plain black dress that covered my boots and a cloak that was heavy with a hood that covered my hair completely. The cloak felt like wool. As I stood there astonished at what I was wearing, two young women approached me. I tucked the shield up under my cloak. I was sure it would cause alarm if the two women saw me holding a Roman shield in the US. As soon as I tucked the shield under my cloak, it seemed to reduce to almost nothing, it did not protrude, and in fact, it was as though it had disappeared.

"Hello," the older of the two young women spoke, "My name is Nya. This is my friend Hynlee. You look lost. Can we help you?"

Nya had dark eyes and dark hair; she appeared to be of Native American or Spanish descent. Hynlee, on the other hand, was Eastern European, with blond hair and blue eyes, probably originally from Holland or possibly Norway, yet she too had features characteristic of a Native American.

As I made this judgment of the two young women, I thought, *Why do we use terms such as these to assess people?* I suspect it results from a mixture of cultures in the US; however, by categorizing people based on appearance, we fall into some very deep misjudgments. Weird how things have crept into our lives without us giving much thought to why we do them.

As I looked over the two, I could see that they were familiar with the area, so I asked, "Where exactly are we?"

Both girls looked at me as if I were from outer space. Hynlee now spoke up, "Are you sure you are okay? That is a very strange question; you are in New York. Did you strike your head or something?" A straightforward young lady not wasting time on nicety; Hynlee was quick to grasp something was not right, and she began to back away from me.

Nya, on the other hand, seemed intrigued by the possibility of an exciting adventure and grabbed Hynlee's hand, forcing her to stand and stopping her retreat. "You do know your name, don't you?" Nya asked.

"Of course I do. My name is Brea. I've been on a journey, and things are a little fuzzy for me right now." Not wanting to scare them or break away from our meeting, I asked where they were coming from.

At that point, Hynlee smiled and said, "A meeting; there is a preacher in our village from New York City. He used to be a lawyer, and we went to hear him."

"Oh," I responded, "And was his message interesting?"

Both young women looked at each other and nodded

yes. Then Nya said, "But something seemed to be missing from his message. He spoke about God, sin, and salvation. In the end, something seemed terribly wrong, though. Instead of encouraging people to seek God, he told them to 'make a decision' to follow God. In fact, he was very insistent that everyone make their decision to believe right then and there."

Hynlee chimed in and said, "He reminded me of one of those store clerks who try to get you to buy something you really don't want to buy. He made those who had made their decision stand up and declare it, while those who did not, he seemed to belittle as if they were wrong and lost if they didn't make their decision to follow God."

I thought to myself, *This must be something important for me to know, or I wouldn't be here.* I turned toward the meeting place the girls had just come from and said, "Is this the first time you've heard something like this?" Both women confirmed never had this type of preaching been heard in these parts. I wasn't sure who this preacher was, but obviously, at least in this place, the message had now changed. All my life, I heard this: Ministers implored people to accept Christ and make their decision to believe. Maybe this was my reason for being here, to find the starting point, the place where things began to change, where believing became a decision made at the moment the preacher told you to make the decision. Based on what Nya and Hynlee were telling me, things were different in the past, and this was a first, at least for them.

I thanked the women for their help and told them I needed to be on my way. I turned and started walking down a path that led away from where the women were heading. As soon as I was out of their sight, my surroundings began to change. I wasn't sure what was happening or where the next part of my journey was going to take me, but now at least, I was a bit wiser about what questions to ask the next time I encountered a local.

I took two steps toward what seemed to be an open doorway, let go of the shield, and suddenly I was back in the Second Chance shop in Chicago. This time I was greeted by Kayla, and something was shining under the old coat she was wearing. If I didn't know better, I would have said it was a sword, but that was nonsense; what would an old woman be doing with a sword?

Kayla greeted me with a smile and said, "Welcome back. Did you discover anything while you were gone?" Apparently, she noticed I had left. I looked deep into her eyes, trying to determine if she was messing with me or if she was genuine.

I said, "Yes, as a matter of fact, I discovered something, although I'm not sure what it meant. It appears, somehow, I was transported back to sometime around 1700-New York, where I met two young women, Nya and Hynlee; they informed me they were just returning from a religious meeting. They said the speaker was a man who used to be a lawyer who came in from New York City. He demanded that the congregation make their decision to accept Jesus and follow God. He then made them stand up and declare their decision. I have no idea what it meant. The young women told me they had never heard such a thing, so perhaps it might have been the beginning of the process most ministers follow today in trying to get people to 'make a decision' to believe."

Kayla smiled that warm, reassuring smile and said, "Some discoveries seem minor at first; however, their impact on the world we live in can completely alter the way things are done." She paused, then asked, "Is there anything else?"

"Well," I started out slowly, trying to formulate my response in a way that made sense of what I was thinking. "Something about the response of those girls seemed puzzling to me. They were alarmed about the way the message at the meeting ended; the message seemed to be laying the burden of salvation on the person making the decision. That worried them." I paused, then continued, "I'm not sure what was bothering them. Today that is the way it is done; people listen to a message and then are implored to 'make a decision.' Once they have made the decision, the minister, or whoever the leader is, declares them a Christian. The women seemed to think there was something missing in that formula, I'm not sure, but I think they felt that minister was leaving God out of the equation."

"And what do you think, Brea?" Kayla asked and then

waited for my response.

"To be honest with you, Kayla, I'm not sure; it is certainly how things are currently done. Hasn't it always been that way?"

"What about people like you, Brea? People who say they can't believe, people who need to put their finger in the nail holes in Jesus' hand. Does the requirement to 'make a decision' create issues for you? If you know so much about it, why haven't you ever made your decision to believe?"

Kayla's question struck deep. I knew why. It was because something inside of me could not believe without proof, because I was broken; whatever it is that allows people to believe without proof, or at least as much as I needed, did not seem to work in me. How many times have I heard a minister or a Christian say, "You just have to take it by faith" or "Accept it; you have all the proof you need right there in the Bible. You do believe the Bible, don't you?"

Right there is the point and the problem. My answer has always been an honest "No, not really!" And that is usually when things get ugly, and I'm judged as a nonbeliever who refuses to believe. The problem is, I simply cannot. Too many things in my life have given rise to doubt when it comes to the Bible's trustworthiness.

In the past, I have always hung my head and responded, "I cannot believe."

Kayla's words broke my thoughts as she said, "Your quest is not over, my child; you have learned something about how things begin. Seldom does the enemy we battle introduce a giant change. It is a slower process, a small move here, a word changes there, and before you know it, the shift has taken place, and no one really notices—at least, the majority do not. Then, someone comes along who challenges the status quo. That person is usually criticized, called odd, and rejected as a heretic. They are told they are different and strange, then cast out from the group. It is the very thing that has created history. Revivals start when someone senses that something is just not right, and they refuse to give in to the majority. It only takes one who is willing to stand up and say, 'This is not right,' so that a false teaching is challenged and can be corrected."

"I think I understand what you are saying. My friends keep trying to get me to accept their teaching, but it seems to fall short of what I need. I've tried to accept things that various groups have told me; however, after a while, their teaching seems to crumble. I find they don't really believe or follow what they are trying to sell me. I finally stopped giving in to them because it is a waste of my time. It does not satisfy," I responded to Kayla after giving it a little thought.

"Do you wish to end this quest, or would you like to continue?" Kayla asked.

At that point, my curiosity started to take over, and

Kayla's words were more of a challenge than a question. "Of course, I want to continue. There must be more to this. Something is missing in my life, and in the preaching today, I want to get to the bottom of this. Besides, the shield is still missing that piece, and I still don't know the name or the word that was written on it. I want to go on. How does this work? I put my hands on the shield, and suddenly it takes me somewhere." I said as I picked up the shield, and sure enough, things changed.

CHAPTER 5
EVIDENCE

As I looked around, the landscape was beautiful, with tall mountains around. I thought to myself, *Those look like the Alps, or it could be somewhere in western Colorado.* Then I saw him, a frumpy little priest. I giggled when I looked at him because he reminded me of the friar in an old movie my grandpa used to watch. However, as he came closer, he resembled an image of Buddha. He approached me and said, "Bless you, my child. You seem unusually happy. Is this a particularly wonderful day for you?"

What could I say? "No, I was laughing at you"? Instead, I responded, "Yes, sir, it is. My name is Brea, and how do I address you?"

At that, my newly found friend smiled and said, "In the past, you would address me as Father Simon; however, I have just converted to a new belief and have resigned from my position. I guess now you can call me Brother

Zachery."

I said, "Would you mind if I simply called you Zach? After all, we are alone, and the formal address seems a bit stuffy."

He smiled a broad smile and said, "I like that idea; it has been a long time since people called me by my birth name, and my sister called me Zach, a sisterly endearment. Once I entered the priesthood, I lost my identity and became someone else. It always bothered me that the name my parents gave me had to be eliminated for me to devote my entire life to the Church. Today I have started on a new journey. No longer am I focused on doing things to gain and maintain my salvation; today, I am living by faith."

"I envy you, Zach. I wish I had the ability to believe and trust without proof, as you do. Sadly, something inside of me seems to be unable to believe." My response caused Zachery's facial expression to change; he seemed to be puzzling over my response.

"Brea, how long have you been in Germany?" Zach asked.

"Not long," I responded. "Why do you ask?"

"Your German accent carries a striking resemblance to that of a Saxon, yet strangely different. I'm just curious."

I nearly fell to the ground. I don't speak German, but apparently, I was doing it. This poor guy was probably detecting my Chicago accent, which impacts and influences people all the way over to Beloit, Wisconsin. How could I ever explain it to him? Instead, I responded, "My heritage is complicated; as a result, there are many dialects and languages I speak, and I'm sure they are impacting my German."

"I suppose it would. Apparently, your training is not in biblical studies, or you would understand the word 'faith.' If you follow the transition of the word faith from the original to our current word, you would know that something is missing from our current word, a third element, if you want to call it that. Without that third element, the word faith has lost much of its power. Faith is supposed to be a shield that protects us against the fiery darts of the enemy; sadly, the Church has become powerless and focused on human effort and lost the third element. Which is one of the reasons I converted and gave up my priesthood," Zach responded.

I looked at him, wanting to ask what that third element was. However, something seemed to be on his mind, so I hesitated. Instead, my question turned to a timeline, and I said, "When was that third element eliminated from the Church?"

He smiled and seemed pleased that I was interested in knowing more. He reminded me of a person who had a lot of deep knowledge about things past and was happy to travel to points of origin and discover truth rather than just simply providing answers. "A guest!" he said, "What a delightful idea, a journey back in time to the place where things changed."

I was shocked. How did he know I was time-traveling? This dream, or whatever it was that I was in, was getting stranger with each journey I took. I looked at him in utter surprise and was just about to say, "How did you know?" when I remembered my encounter with Nya and Hynlee and their reaction to my questions, so instead, I simply said, "What do you mean?"

"In my dwelling, I have many incunabula. If you would journey to my home, I can share them with you, and together we can go on a knowledge quest. I find answers are more fulfilling when we discover and experience them rather than being told. Understanding tends to be driven deeper when discovered on a quest. Knowledge quests are exciting; I've gone on many of them. We will travel from our current year, 1530, back in time through the writings I have accumulated. It will be such a pleasant journey, and it requires so little walking. Sometimes I tire easily, and my feet hurt. We can settle down with a nice brew and start our journey back in time to the year of our Lord, 1200."

Interesting. Without asking, he just told me the year is 1530 and in Germany. Incunabula told me he was steeped in the old ways even though he was a new convert to a new teaching. The word book had started making its way into the mainstream by 1530. I am not that in tune with religious history; however, I am aware that Martin Luther posted his

95 Theses in 1517. It appears the movement has caught up to this former priest. But why 1200? That seemed like a question I could ask, and so I did. "Zach, why 1200? What is so magical about that year?"

"Well," Zach responded, "That is when the third change took place that set the stage for our current understanding of Faith."

After a short walk, we arrived at Zach's dwelling, a small cottage nestled in the side of a hill; while primitive by the standards of my time, it was cozy and quaint. I felt like I had just stepped into a movie about the past. Zach pointed me to a wooden stool, and with that, he grabbed a couple of parchments from a shelf in his cottage and sat them on the table. He then proceeded to place two wicker cups on the table and poured some liquid into them from a leather wine skin, which he had just filled from a small wooden barrel. He placed one in front of me and the other in front of his place at the table and sat down.

As he was preparing these things, I thought, *A clue, another place in time. I was sure I would be whisked back at that very moment, but instead, I was still where I had been, in 1530 Germany with Zach, the former priest. It appeared my reason for being here was not over. Was there something more to this? Did I dare say anything to Zach about my quest? What could possibly happen if I were to say something to him about the shield and my quest? After all, this journey was about as weird as it could get. I couldn't see any way it could get weirder.*

I pulled the shield out from under my cloak and said, "Zach, I am on a time-travel quest to discover the missing name or word on this shield. At some point in time, the shield lost its name, and when it did, it also lost its power. I am from many centuries in the future, and it appears my business here is not done, or I would not still be here. Now, we could sit here in your home and read your books, or we could try to travel to another place and time and discover what your books would tell you."

Zach immediately stood up and took a couple of steps back, stared at me briefly, then snatched up a parchment with something handwritten on it. I was sure he was going to run away, thinking me either to be crazy or a witch. Instead, after a moment, he sat back down and stared at me, then pushed the parchment my way. When he finally opened his mouth, he said, "I had a vision that I would meet someone who needed me to guide them. The person I was to help needed to find something that was lost. I wrote my vision down on this parchment so I would not forget. I never expected something this strange. How can this be? How can you possibly be from the future, and why should I believe you?"

I could empathize with Zach; I have asked that same question, "Why should I believe you?" many times over when people have tried to get me to believe their words about God, religion, and salvation. Their appeals all seemed like a mist or a vapor quickly disappearing into thin air. I guess the poor little former priest needed some sort of evidence to prove that I was telling the truth. The fact that I was carrying a Roman shield should have been enough, but I guessed my frumpy new friend needed more. Then I remembered my purse, which was still hidden under my cloak. I pulled it out and grabbed my cell phone. Of course, I couldn't place a call, but it had a light on it, and the material it was made of was not from 1530. I held it up in front of Zach and said, "Here, Zach, this is a device from the future. It allows me to have conversations with people far away from me. Take it in your hand, hold it, and feel the smooth, hard texture. Those numbers are buttons; press them and see what happens. This device, in my time, is a library with millions of books, maps, and images for me to view. If I have a question, I can simply enter the question, and my device, called a cell phone, will display the answer. I can read it like a book, or it will read it to me."

With that, Zach pulled his hands back away from me and said, "I do not require touching the thing. It is enough evidence to convince me of what you say. My vision did not prepare me for this, and yet my life has. I would ask one thing of you, though."

"Sure, Zach; what is it?" I responded.

"Why, if your device can provide you with the answers to all your questions, are you here? Why didn't you simply ask the device?"

My little Buddha-looking friend had a valid point, why was I here? I thought for a moment and then remembered his own words and said, "I believe you already provided me with the answer; discovery and experience, Zach. Whatever my future holds seems to require the answer to my quest to go much deeper, perhaps to that place where convictions are developed. It would seem I need something more profound than just an answer, something far deeper that can satisfy and resolve my belief issue."

With that, Zachery said, "What must I do?"

I had no idea where to go from here. I was time-traveling with a shield; would it work for him? So many questions, so much out of control, all of this was so unlike me, my security resulting from control was faltering; for a moment, I felt panic, and my walls began to collapse around me, then I remembered Kayla and her assuring me she would be with me. But where was she? I needed her to make this decision for me. What if Zachery came with me? Would it disrupt time? *Kayla, where are you? I need you*, I thought. Then, I remembered all I had to do was let go of the shield, and I would be back in the Second Chance shop. I started to release, but as I did, Zach began to fade. I stopped instantly and tightened my grip on the shield, clinging to it so my new friend would not leave me. Strange, I barely knew him, and here I was, afraid of losing him. So many friends in the past were cast off like a used container, and here I was, clinging to one I barely knew.

How different this new friend was; he wasn't judging me like all the other friends in my life. Then it struck me; maybe the other people in my life weren't judging me either; maybe, just maybe, I was judging them. In my past—his future—I was always looking for the faults in people. Why was that? Why did I always feel it was my duty or responsibility to point out other people's faults?

Zachery shook me back to the moment and said, "Brea, how are we going to travel?"

I had no idea if what I was about to tell him would work or not. I felt we had to give it a try, so I said, "Take hold of my shield, and don't let go." He did as I asked, and sure enough, we were suddenly standing in a place I had never been before. I said, "I wonder where we are... More than that, I wonder when we are."

Zachery was delighted, he looked around, and in the distance, he saw a sight that resembled a place he had visited once a long time ago. He smiled and announced, "I believe we are in France."

His confidence in where we were was high. I asked him how he knew, and he responded, "Those towers at the harbor entrance, I remember them as a child. We are in France, but the real question is, when? The towers look the same, but something is different, almost primitive. It appears we might be sometime in the early 1200s. I was planning on arriving here through a book, but this is far more exciting."

I was perplexed. Why would we be here, and why this time? What was the third change Zach mentioned? At that point, I realized I needed an answer, and I felt Kayla might have what I needed. Without thinking, I released the shield and was instantly back in the Second Chance store. To my horror, I was there without Zachery. In an instant, I realized I had lost my friend, literally lost him. Was he stuck in 1200 France? Or was he back in his time? Kayla was aware when I left. Did Zach know I was gone? I felt horrible. What had I done? Time-travel mode was confusing. One simple mistake and I possibly ruined a friendship and left that friend in his past; how could I have been so foolish? Why didn't I think of my friend? What I did impacted him; why was it always about me? Maybe Zach knew why we were there, and maybe he could have answered my question. Instead, without thinking, I turned loose of the shield and our friendship. Why did I do that?

Then it dawned on me. I've been doing that all my life, developing a friendship, and then suddenly doing something selfish that cost me my friends and even my relationship with my family members. But why? Why would I keep doing that?

Then a thought came; Zach didn't let go. I had, so maybe he was still there. Maybe, if I grabbed the shield, it would take me back to him. I had to take a chance; I had to fix this; I couldn't afford to lose my frumpy little Buddha-looking

Zachery. Even though what I was about to do might fail, I had to do it. I forced myself to take the chance and said out loud, "This friendship is worth taking a chance and trying to fix this." With that, I grabbed the shield, and everything changed. I was once again in the same spot I had left. To my amazement, Zach was staring right at me with a big smile on his face. I grabbed him, gave him a big hug, and said, "I am so sorry I let go."

Zachery smiled, hugged me back, and said, "It is okay, Brea. I knew you would come back around. I figured, when you disappeared, if I kept holding on, you would return." Then he said something I would never forget "Brea, in my life, I have found that not all friends stay with you. Sometimes, when you make choices, it causes others to break away from you. When I left the Church and began to follow a new path, many of my friends cut me off; they didn't understand. They thought that excommunicating me would cause me to change. Kind of a "tough love" type of move. When they did this, I could have reacted poorly and become angry with them, but then that would have been doing to them what they had done to me. Instead, I followed the rule of Jesus 'Do unto others as you would have them do unto you.' We find those words in the Gospel of Matthew, chapter 7, verse 12. I knew that if I believed in you and held on to the shield, sooner or later, you would return. Had I let go, I would have returned to my own time like you just did, but then I would have missed out on the rest of our quest and would never see you again. You are my friend. I didn't want to lose you, so even though you let go, I held on with the hope you would return, I am here for you, and you believe me, don't you?"

The tears were flowing, and I was a mess. How could I not believe him? The *evidence* was undeniable. He was there; he held on and waited for me to correct my mistake; he believed in me. "Yes, my dear friend, I do believe!" For the first time in a very long time, something inside of me started working, my believer ignited, and I believed. Instantly I blurted out, "Could this be the missing piece? Could *evidence* be the name that was on the shield?" I looked at the space in the shield that was missing, and to my amazement, the letters "ST" suddenly appeared on the shield. That is weird. Evidence isn't spelled with ST.

Zach could see the confusion on my face. He said, "Brea, your quest is not over; my work here is nearly done. In my vision, I was only to help you to a certain point, and I am afraid this is that point for now. Is there anything you need to ask me that I can answer for you?"

I was heartbroken to think my new friend would now leave me, yet we would be parting friends, and I'm not sure time can end that. Friends come and go in your life, but the important thing is to part as friends and not as enemies. This was probably the first time in my life that was about to happen, and while I was sad over the parting, there was joy in my heart, knowing we would be friends forever. Knowing Zach was right, I had peace deep in my heart;

however, that didn't mean my eyes were cooperating; we were both tearful. I said, "Why here and why this time?"

"Because, Brea," Zachery began to speak words that showed so much wisdom. I saw my friend in a different light. "This is where a very small change took place that is important to your quest. Based on the letters that appeared on the shield, I could tell you what the name is, but would you understand? Would it provide your shield with power, or would it simply be another word? *Knowledge that lacks personal experience is simply doctrine.* It is like the Law; it is the letter that kills. Add experience and knowledge has life and power. The word you are seeking, in part, means *evidence*, but it means more than that, and you need to discover the other parts of the word. This quest has helped me answer some questions that I, too, have been struggling with, and now that I realize this part of the puzzle, I now know the secret. Your journey is not over; in this time and in this language, the word 'faith' began to develop. It comes from the French word *fied*, which means fidelity and trust. That word has to do with our faithfulness to God and the family of God or our religious fervor. It was here that the name on the shield was further removed, but this is not where that first change took place. It simply buried deeper the truth revealed in the name, making it harder to see. The name on the shield is much older than this, and you will need to go back even further to discover what you are looking for."

After a long and sad yet joyful goodbye, Zachery began

to release the shield. As he did, I heard him say, "Brea Rea Joyce." How remarkable that this person, five hundred years older than me, knew my name. Or was he telling me to rejoice? Either way, his impact on my life would live on.

As I was reflecting on this moment and watched him fade away, I realized I should talk to Kayla at this point, so I released the shield, and I was back in the Second Chance store.

Kayla was right there waiting for me; she never left. I wondered how long I had been gone. I asked Kayla, "How long was I gone?"

Kayla responded, "I was barely able to heat the water for my tea. It appears you discovered something; I see the letters ST on the shield; that means you are making progress."

"You wouldn't believe what just happened!" I nearly shouted my response; I think, at that moment, I was happier than I had been in a long time, and yet I lost my friend. Wait, that is not true. I did not lose a friend; I gained one. "I met an ex-priest in 1530; he was amazing. He is part of the reason for the ST on the shield; he gave me evidence of his friendship even after I made a terrible mistake."

"It was nice to see Brother Zachery," Kayla stated.

"What, you know him? Did you see him? How is that possible?" I nearly shouted. Who was this woman, and how could she possibly know Zach?

"Brea," Kayla responded, "I told you I would be with you and never leave you. Just because you cannot always see me, it does not mean I am not there. We are connected in ways you do not yet perceive; however, you will soon enough. I believe you have someone waiting for you. Take the shield, child, and be on your way."

She knew. She was there with me even though I could not see her. My belief in Kayla and her friendship increased with this new piece of evidence. I thought to myself, *There it is again, that word evidence. In my lifelong struggle to believe, how had I missed such an important part of believing?* As I was thinking this, I took hold of the shield again. I wondered where it would take me next. Suddenly, I was back in the exact spot I left just moments earlier. Only Zachery was gone.

CHAPTER 6

SEARCH FOR THE SWORD

This was odd. Why was I in the 1200s France? Zachery had already revealed that the meaning of the name on the shield was further buried in this time by the introduction of the French word Fied, which was further buried by the English word Faith, both meaning fidelity to a thing. Neither explains what it is that produces belief or fidelity. Both words center on us doing something. Is it any wonder that people centuries later have difficulty understanding the concept that the original writers intended?

In my line of work, this is not unusual. You must understand the impact certain things have on different societies. If you were in a primitive country, for example, and used a word that in the USA represented quality, like a car brand, or a particular type of clothing, to describe quality in the primitive country, your message would be lost. It appears a similar thing has happened with the word "faith." The French and English used a word in their language that was like a word in a different language, that meant what they perceived to be the same or close to the same thing; while that word did not have the same meaning, it conveyed what they perceived to be the same thing or similar. Greek, for example, has multiple words to describe love. In English, there is one word, and the meaning is determined by the situation in which the word is used.

Once that word is used over and over, it becomes a tradition. When that word is used by someone in authority, such as a college professor, high-ranking government official, respected religious leader, or even a media figure, those who respect the individual, or the office this person holds, begin to use the word to convey an idea. Many Sunday school teachers have taught the idea that the word "justification" meant "just as if I never sinned." After that, the pupils began to repeat that phrase as the definition, and the word began to mean what the teacher taught to those who followed such teacher. I'm sure the teacher was not the first to use the phrase, they probably heard it from another person that they respected, and once done, that phrase became the definition of the word "Justification" for thousands—if not millions—of people.

The truth about the actual definition of the word we translate as "justification" is that the Greek word used by those who wrote the New Testament had a twofold meaning; the first, to *pardon*, and the second, to *accept*.

While the more popular and more recent traditional teaching would leave a person with the idea that they were innocent, the true meaning does not allow a false sense of our own righteousness but a state of forgiveness received as the result of mercy or payment made on our behalf by another. In the case of the Christian religion, the state of justification is the result of the payment made by Jesus on our behalf. Christians say Jesus is our sacrifice, or the price paid for our salvation.

It is this very idea that presents a problem for me and those like me. I cannot come to a place where I believe that this price has been paid and that by it, I am justified in the sense that I am both pardoned and accepted by God. I have been told by virtually everyone I've met that I need to accept Christ as the sacrifice and payment for my sins. However, that is where the "disconnection" comes in. I can't! Every time I've tried, I end with the same frustration when challenged by that inner voice, or the next morning reality sets in. I feel just as guilty as the day before, just as unfulfilled as I was before I made my decision to accept Christ.

My friends or those around me who have tried to mentor me keep telling me, "You just have to believe and stand on your decision!" To me, this has always smacked my works, which is contrary to what the Bible says about the entire matter. If salvation is based on what I do, i.e., my decision, then it is a matter of works, not grace.

Please understand this, the issue with tradition over truth is not isolated to the Christian religion. The same thing happens in all walks of life, from archeology to math; traditional teaching has always stood in the way of truth. There are other things that have worked their way into our minds as truth that may not be so.

For example, we have been taught the Pyramids of Egypt were the tombs of the Pharaohs. There are those who question and challenge this. Our belief that this was the purpose of the Pyramids is based on a bias of history that has been repeated over and over throughout the ages. That bias might cause us to completely miss the real purpose of those great structures.

The Bible is another one of those traditions that have caused a great deal of error. Depending on you and your culture, the Bible means different things. To some, it is simply a collection of writings. To others, it is the "Word of God." Even within communities that utilize the Bible, there are different views. To some, only the first five books of the Old Testament make up the Bible. To others, only the New Testament does; and still, others view the entire Bible as the authoritative word of God. Who is right? Or are any of them right?

Standing by the gate of the harbor, as I was thinking through all of this, someone walked up behind me. I didn't notice him at first; in fact, he snuck up on me like some type of 13th-century Ninja, dressed in battle garb that I instantly recognized as that worn by the young soldier who was standing next to me on the battlefield during my first encounter with the shield.

I turned to greet him, but he instantly turned away from me. At first, I thought he was shy, so I introduced myself. "Hello, my name is Brea Rea Joyce." In the past, I seldom used my full name when introducing myself, but now after my adventure with Zach, it felt natural, and for the first time, I felt like I was living up to my name, at least in part. However, the young soldier seemed to not hear me. I thought to myself, *I wonder if he is deaf.* I spoke up a little louder, "Hello, my name is Brea Rea Joyce. What is your name?" He still didn't respond. Then I said, "Can you not hear me, or can you not understand me?" I thought perhaps the translator thing on this shield wasn't working. After all, it was missing a piece, and Kayla said it had lost its power.

Suddenly the young soldier spoke, "No, madam, I am not deaf; and yes, I understand you. However, I am a Templar Knight, and we do not communicate or have contact with women. It is part of our code."

"Really?" I responded. "Did I approach you, or did you approach me? If I recall correctly, I was standing here minding my own business, and you walked up to me; if you don't want to talk to me, why did you approach me?"

Apologetically he replied, "You are right, I did approach you, and you have every right to challenge my intentions and my inconsistency. Last night when I was in my barracks, I had a dream. In that dream, there was a woman dressed in a red cloak, like the one you are wearing."

I looked down and realized I was wearing a red cloak. To be honest, I hadn't noticed what I was wearing. Now that he said that, I realized I was wearing a red cape, the boots were still my own, but now my attire had changed again and was matching something worn in this time period. Not the ruffled, huge hooped dress that you might have seen in the movies, mine was more in line with a woman who was very conservative, rode horseback, worked in the fields, or something that demanded a more modest and realistic attire. I said to the young Templar, "Okay, that explains part of your approach; however, it does not explain what you want."

"Madam, I am very sorry for my abruptness. I simply wasn't sure how to approach you, me a stranger and you a young woman alone standing by the harbor gate to our city. To approach you at all is so far from what I have been taught. Under these conditions, it is, even in a social setting, most inexcusable," the Templar responded.

I felt sorry for him when I realized how embarrassed he was and realized it took a lot of courage for him to break with the code he had committed to. That, however, did not answer my question; he still hadn't told me what he wanted. I felt we were getting off on the wrong foot with this conversation, so I changed it up a little and made it sound more sympathetic to his situation, and said, "I have introduced myself. Please tell me what they call you; certainly, you have a name. You are not just known by Knight!"

At that, the Templar cracked a smile and said, "No, madam, my given name is Kolby. I am in a special unit of the Templars, and I have the ability to approach people with little or no notice of my approach."

"Nice to meet you, Kolby," I replied, "that explains your Ninja approach."

"What kind of approach?" Kolby questioned.

"Ninja… It is a word used where I come from. It means you are able to approach people without them noticing," I said, then asked again, "What is it I can do for you?"

"I actually like that word; it is more efficient than 'able to approach without you noticing' That is what I will call myself going forward, 'Kolby the Ninja,'" Kolby mused.

I had to laugh. Wouldn't it be funny if this was where the word was first used, and now I was responsible for introducing it? Then I realized I needed to be careful; this kind of change to history could disrupt a lot of future things. Ninja might suddenly become a French word instead of a Japanese word that finds its roots in Chinese; that is, of course, provided all of this was real. I still wasn't sure.

"The reason for my approach," Kolby continued, "is

that I have been searching for something that seems to be lost in the life I have chosen. I speak words, words written in books I have read. Our code is based on many of those words. However, those words have no meaning to me. The path the Templars are taking seems off. There are things going on within our organization that are very different from what I believe scripture directs. I feel like we have lost the sword, which is sharper than a two-edged blade. In my dream, the red-capped woman assisted me by inviting me on her quest. Are you on a quest, and why are you standing alone at the harbor?"

"I have no idea why I am here unless it is to help you. Believe it or not, Kolby, I am on a quest. You will find this very difficult to believe, but I am not from this time. If you travel with me on this quest, you will time-travel into the past. Do you believe me?" I asked.

"Such words are foolishness, Miss Brea; certainly, no one could travel through time. I have traveled over deserts and mountains, and each of them took time away from my life, but none gave it back. To think we could go back in time and not forward is pure fantasy."

Here we go again, I thought to myself. How do I convince him? Should I pull out my phone again?" That seemed like something I would have done in the past to prove myself, but suddenly I thought of something, and the conversation in my head went like this: *Is there a better way, Brea? What if you ask him what he needs as proof and fulfill that need? A friend doesn't dictate; they assist. Kolby needs to understand and needs evidence.* With those thoughts, I asked, "Kolby, what can I do to prove my words are true?"

"Do you have something from your time that I do not have in mine? Perhaps something that cannot possibly come from my time, some form of art or a tool, which can prove your words. I need evidence."

There was that word *evidence* again; no doubt evidence is important when it comes to belief. One of the things I am learning during this quest is the evidence that convinces one person is not the same as the evidence that convinces another. I realized that if I showed Kolby my cell phone, he might think me to be a witch; however, if I provided something that he requested, he might be convinced of the truth. I thought for a moment... Art or a tool. I had both in my bag; I opened it and drew out my wallet, which had photos in it. I also pulled out my wristwatch; I was sure he had no access to these in his time. I handed him the watch and said, "Here, Kolby, is a timepiece from my time; the writing on it is a new version of English, and we use that language in a country called the United States of America. My country has not been discovered by Europeans yet; soon, though, it will be discovered by the Spanish. As you can see, it is a tool for telling time. It is what we call digital, and notice the date is in the future. Also, in my wallet or purse, I have photos; these are images captured on a tool called a camera. With that tool, we can capture in an instant what it takes an artist many hours, if not years, to create. Is that enough proof for you? I have more if you need it. I have a tool with me that can capture your image if you would like."

I could see Kolby was mesmerized by what he was looking at. A huge smile came across his face; he felt at ease. I could see the tension falling away from his face. It was as if he, for the first time in a long time, believed the words of an individual, not simply because of the words spoken but because of the *evidence* presented.

"Thank you, Brea, this is amazing. I am ready to follow you. Where are we going? Will we find what I am looking for there?"

"I have no idea where we are going or when in the past we will be going to, Kolby, but wherever and whenever it is, we will go together." With that, I removed the shield from under my cloak and held it out in front of him. His eyes widened. To think a woman would possess a shield of such quality. Women simply did not carry a battle shield with them, but this one did.

As I thought about our journey, it dawned on me that it might be easier to travel if I could share the shield with my new traveling companion. I reached up near the place where the nameplate was missing. There was a small portion of it that was jagged and thin, and I was able to break a piece off and hand it to Kolby. I said, "I'm not sure if this will work, but I would like to try an experiment if you are willing." He agreed. I continued, "This shield takes me to the time and place I need to be. If you are to travel with me, you simply take hold of the shield, and we go. However, it restricts your movement; you are very dependent on me. I would like to try this and see if it provides you with more freedom; you will always have a little piece of my shield with you. If we become separated, it might allow you to move on with your quest and or return to your time."

At that, Kolby's eyes widened, and he pointed to the shield. The piece I broke off and handed to him suddenly grew back where I had broken it off. Kolby, still holding his piece in his hand, was astonished and said, "Is that how things work in your time?"

I was just as astonished as he was; a self-healing shield, who would have thought? Why didn't it simply heal itself of the nameplate? Then I remembered what Kayla said, "It is not broken; it is lost." I realized that the missing piece was something I needed to discover; perhaps in another place and time, the shield was intact. I replied, "No, Kolby, it does not. There are a lot of things you and I will see that are not normal, and this is one of them."

As I thought about how we could travel together, I thought perhaps if we held hands, we would be moving as one. After handing him a piece of the shield, I instructed him, saying, "Take hold of my hand, and we will be on our way."

At that, he backed away and said, "I cannot; our code forbids contact with women!"

I said, "Really, that is how things are going to be? Your 'code' prevents it? Didn't you tell me your code was faulty and you were seeking answers? Maybe you need to let go of your 'rules and regulations' that restrict rather than free you, and perhaps then you will begin to discover the truth."

Kolby lowered his head and said, "You are right, Brea. I have been so focused on pleasing those who have set these rules over me that it has blinded me. As a result, I have forgotten what it means to follow my heart, and with regard to this, my heart is telling me to go with you. If this means breaking away from my doctrinal dogma, then I must."

With that, my new friend took hold of my hand, and our environment changed instantly. Something about this place seemed familiar; although newer than I recalled, it still seemed more primitive than my memory of it. Rome, yes, that was it; we were in Rome. This was certainly an interesting change from France to Rome in an instant. I wish I could get around Chicago like this, a five-mile drive in Chicago traffic can take an hour, especially if it is downtown during rush hour, and now we just traveled some 1,000-plus miles instantly. Kolby and I looked around at our surroundings. There, in the distance, was the coliseum; you could hear shouts coming from it. Chances were good; we were sometime prior to 400 CE since around 404, the emperor Honorius banned the games, but why here and why now? Kolby was looking for a sword, I was looking for a name for my shield, and this didn't make any sense to me at all.

As I began to assess our time, I noted Kolby's heavy Templar armor had changed to a tunic, strapped boots, a *lorica segmentata* (upper body armor worn by Roman officers), and a helmet of a Roman soldier of very high rank. He had a shield and sword strapped to his back. Whatever he wore under it must have still been intact because he didn't notice the change. However, he did notice my change in attire, and he commented, "Brea, your clothing has been altered. You are wearing a tunic and strapped boots, you have your shield strapped to your back, and now your upper portion no longer has a hooded cape, you are now covered with a *lorica segmentata,* and a Roman helmet covers your head."

I thought, *How funny that he could see the changes in me but was oblivious to the changes he had gone through. But then that is the way it seems to go; we seldom realize how we ourselves have changed, only the changes in others. I wonder if that explains some of our judgments of those around us.*

I said, "Kolby, I'm going to leave you for a moment, but if you have a piece of my shield, things should remain the same for you. I will be back before you know it. Will you wait for me?"

Kolby nodded his approval, and with that, I turned loose of the shield. Instantly I was back in my own time and in Kayla's shop. How long had I been gone? It must have been a day or two. Suddenly I felt the need to use the restroom. This was odd. I wondered how long I had really been gone, if there was a restroom here in this store, and if it really was a store.

Suddenly, Kayla came into view; there was a glow about her and something shining under her coat, which she quickly covered. Kayla instantly diverted my attention away from what I saw by saying, "Tell me where you have been and what did you learn?"

I was hesitant to ask about the restroom, but nature was calling, and I needed to ask. Kayla instinctively pointed to the sign near the rear of the store, which displayed the word "Restroom." After completing this urgent task, I returned to Kayla. She was now sitting in a chair near the spot where the shield again hung on the display rack.

I started our conversation with the words, "This is so strange, Kayla. I'm not sure how long I had been gone, but it appears long enough for natural things to occur. In this time, it seems like moments; in shield time, it seems like a couple of days, but my body clock tells me it has been a few hours." It was more of a question than a statement.

Kayla responded, "Time is an interesting concept, Brea. It holds most of the world captive by its limitations. You do realize that time is merely a concept and not a reality, don't you?"

"I guess I never thought about it, to be honest with you." My response startled me a little; in the past, I would have tried to disguise my lack of knowledge of a subject. I'm not sure why I did that. I suppose it had something to do with control. When we must receive from others, we are at their mercy, and for me, I could not willingly submit to another. However, things were beginning to change in my heart and life. The past few minutes, hours, or whatever time this quest had taken were beginning to bring change to my life. I'm sure my thoughts took only a fraction of a second, and I continued, "Please explain to me what you mean."

"Well," Kayla said, "time is merely a word that describes a series of events, such as the sun rising and setting. We use a twenty-four-hour clock positioned where we are to determine time in that location. However, if you were to move that clock to another planet, for example, with greater gravity, that clock in that place would still show a twenty-four-hour cycle; however, back on Earth with less gravity, several days, weeks, months, and years would pass. This is true of not only clocks but events. Your conscious mind is very limited in what it can process in a second; your subconscious mind, on the other hand, can process many millions of times per second more data than your conscious mind. If your conscious mind were to receive a list of all the things your subconscious mind processed, based on the conscious mind's limited ability, it would say all those events took several days or perhaps months or longer to accomplish. However, the subconscious accomplished all those things in a second. Time is not real; it is relative; it is simply a concept formulated in the past to provide placeholders. History is not real; it is simply information held in a place. Once you know how to travel to that place, you can pull the information out at will and revisit it as often as you like."

"Wow, that is a lot to grasp, Kayla," I spouted out. "I would have challenged you if I had not just experienced exactly what you are telling me. If I understand you correctly, by taking hold of the shield, I am simply opening a file with the information recorded on a file in that place. The file is in a place, and with the shield, I can go to the file, open the file as I would on my computer, retrieve the file, travel to where the information is recorded, and retrieve it now and whenever I choose to. Is this what you are telling me?"

"Very good, Brea. You catch on fast," Kayla replied. "If you choose, you can return to any of these places as often as you like because that information is recorded there; visiting people, places, and even events is as simple as pulling a file from a folder hidden in your subconscious. The trick is to know how to travel to where the file is stored."

"Are you telling me everything that ever was, always is?" I questioned.

"My dear, there is a being called 'I Am' who knows not only what was but what is and what will be. When you are part of I Am's family, you have access to all that belongs to I Am. Knowledge is only one of the benefits."

"Okay, Kayla, this is beginning to sound like a Bible class or something." I regretted speaking those words before I finished saying them.

Kayla winked, a smile crossed her face, and she said, "Brea, when you know you are a daughter of the King, you can ask whatever you want, and it will be given to you."

"I've been told that in the past; however, whenever I've asked for something, it doesn't come to me. I don't believe in that stuff because it doesn't happen in real life, only Bible fantasy."

"Ah, but here we are, and we are here in response to your cry for help in this matter," Kayla responded. "Your argument is false based on the reality of this moment, for you did ask, and now this quest is the answer to your request. Perhaps your real issue does not stem from not believing things said in the Bible; rather, it is the result of you not knowing you are a daughter of I Am? If you knew you were, then you would know whatever you ask; you can have because you ask with faith, believing they will come to you. The key is faith, but what is it? Once you have discovered faith, those things you would ask would be given to you, pressed down, shaken together, and overflowing."

I dropped my head and sadly responded, "No doubt, Kayla, I do not believe I am a daughter of I Am. In fact, I'm not sure I Am is real. After all, what evidence do I have that a God really exists?"

There was that word *evidence* again. It was forcing its way into my every thought; I knew from the *evidence* of the restoration on the shield that it was a part of the missing piece. While it was partially the answer, it did not seem to be the complete answer; something was still missing. "Kayla," I said, "evidence seems to be playing an important role in what I am looking for. Yet it does not appear to be the entire answer or thing that is missing. I base that on the fact that my quest is not over and that the name is only partially restored. There is more to this, isn't there?"

"You have answered your own question, haven't you, my dear?" Kayla replied. "Something else is puzzling you; what is it?"

It was as if she could read my mind, and I saw no reason to hold back, so I said, "The shield, I broke a piece off and gave it to another person, a Templar Knight I am currently traveling with. I thought it might provide him with some stability in our journey and might even help him along his own quest. As soon as I broke it off and gave it to him, it grew back. I thought that was strange."

"Why should that seem strange to you, Brea?" Kayla

questioned, "After all, the shield is faith, and faith once shared is not less; rather, it remains the same and grows."

"The shield is faith?" I nearly shouted, "What do you mean it is faith?"

Kayla smiled and said, "My dear, the faith you hold is missing something. You are here to find that missing piece. Take another look at the shield; examine it closely. Do you see something different?"

To be honest, I hadn't really examined it since I looked at it with Zach. I was so busy with this new way of traveling and the things I was learning I hadn't taken the time to look at it. I paused and took a good look at the shield; sure enough, something had changed. The area where the name was missing had apparently started filling in, not only with the letters ST, but the space between the letters was filling in; it was as if I had discovered more of the missing piece. So, it was true, part of what was missing from faith, or at least my faith, was *evidence*.

Excitement welled up in my chest. "Kayla," I chimed, "more of the shield is restored!"

Kayla smiled and said, "I hope this encourages you to go on with your quest, not out of curiosity, but of need to know. By the way, isn't someone waiting for you?"

I nearly forgot my traveling companion Kolby; with that, I reached up and took the shield in hand and was instantly back in ancient Rome.

CHAPTER 7

WHAT IS IN A NAME?

There, standing in front of me, was Kolby. However, we were not where we were when I left; we were in the coliseum. His *lorica segmentata* was now dented and scrapped, his helmet showed marks as if it had protected his head from a blow from some sort of weapon, his shield was off his back, and the sword was in his hand, clinched and ready for war. Yet there was a smile on his face. It appeared he had won some type of conflict. I wasn't sure what had taken place in my absence, but my feisty Ninja Knight's Templar had busied himself with something in my absence. Then I noticed the crowd cheering as if a gladiator had triumphed.

"What have you been up to?" I asked.

"I heard a commotion here in the coliseum and wandered over to see what was going on." Kolby nearly shouted with excitement and to be heard over the roar of the crowd. "Somehow, I entered where the gladiators enter, and I found myself confronted by some creature I had never seen before but sensed I had done battle with. I drew my sword and shield. While it was not the sharpest sword, it did provide me with a weapon to use against the beast, my training in warfare allowed me to successfully fend off the attacks of the beast; the shield appears to be the one you provided me, it allowed me to block some of the beast's blows, the *lorica segmentata* deflected the rest. It appears that to fight in this arena, you need full armor. While the shield was not complete, it did provide me with some protection. This entire challenge showed me what is missing from my time. The sword, which is the Word of God, is missing something, and I must find it."

I was crying as I hugged my Ninja Knight. The happiness that I experienced knowing that I was in some way helping my friend find what his heart needed, created a joy inside of me I cannot describe. It was impossible to speak it. I wondered if this was what the Bible talked about when it said Joy is unspeakable. Probably not, but it was great knowing that my new friend had also found a piece that was missing from his life. "Funny, Kolby, a short time ago, you wouldn't even take my hand, and yet now you let me hug you," I said as I hugged him.

Kolby's eyes were flashing light as if he could see for the first time in his life. "You," he said, "are not just a woman; you are my sister and a fellow soldier. My rules do

What Is in a Name?

not prohibit such contact."

He smiled when he said it, so I wasn't sure if he was kidding or serious. However, he was right. When I hugged him, it was not as if I were just hugging a man, but a brother, a team member. We were united under one banner seeking our truth. Then I remembered my first encounter with the shield, there was a sword, and it was missing the pummel. How strange that I was so self-absorbed in my quest that I missed what another person needed in theirs. Perhaps that is what caused those around me to miss what I was looking for; they were so busy trying to tell me what helped them they couldn't see what I needed. Then it hit me; maybe they could not help me because they did not know what was available to help me. "What was that beast you battled, and where is it, Kolby?"

"I wounded it, Brea, but did not kill it. The beast suddenly turned to smoke and disappeared like the steam from a pot over the fire." Kolby seemed mystified by such a turn of events. "I nearly forgot what happened. The beast vanished, the crowd began to cheer, and all I could think about was victory. Small as it was, it was still a victory." Suddenly his emotions changed, and he said, "Could it be that all of this was exposing the weakness in the armor of God we are using to fight the enemy in my time and yours?"

I realized, as he said it, that might be the problem with all of Christianity in my time. If an enemy wanted to defeat an opponent, radical change would more likely be met with greater resistance; however, a subtle change here and there, a small piece removed unnoticed, could happen slowly over time. A slightly less than complete victory might not be seen as a big deal, much like Kolby's battle in the coliseum that had just taken place, the crowd saw an enemy slain, but the person in the battle knew it was not a complete victory, for he did not slay the opponent, he simply wounded it and sensed the problem was in the armor and weapons he was using. While the crowd of spectators ignorantly cheered what they perceived as a victory, the individual in the battle knew it was not.

Hmm, I thought to myself, *if the crowd never experienced more than a superficial victory, then when someone else had that same superficial victory, the crowd would cheer because they knew nothing better.* I realized this might very well be what was happening in Christian churches around the world, not only in my day but in Kolby's as well. How deep did this thing go? I suddenly became aware that what the Bible says about Satan is so incredibly true; he is the father of lies, deceptive and cunning. If he planted some of these seeds along the way so many hundreds of years ago, their roots were running deep, and it was going to be a real battle trying to weed them out. By the time many of these things reached my time, after centuries of traditional teaching, they were not challenged by those who were listening.

Instantly I recalled my first intentional journey into the past, the two young women, Nya and Hynlee. I remembered

What Is in a Name?

the conversation; at that moment in time, there was a slight turn from the truth to something less powerful. It was barely noticeable by those in attendance. However, both young ladies recognized a shift, and it bothered them. That subtle change that began in their time impacted those in my time; what Nya and Hynlee saw as an unsettling change and departure from truth in their time, in my time, was taught and practiced as truth. Hundreds of years passed, and it was now standard practice, to the point that the crowd cheered at each less-than-complete victory because it was all they had ever known. Could it be that this deception started even further back than the fourth century?

Here we were sometime prior to 400, and already the crowd was cheering at an incomplete victory; already, the deception had taken hold.

Immediately Kolby and I were whisked to another place and time, earlier but not by much. The two of us stood in a small room in what appeared to be a church or meeting place. There, before us, were two priests counting out coins, probably from collections at a recent religious service. The priests were startled by our sudden appearance, and while not completely alarmed by the sudden appearance of two people dressed in Roman officer uniforms, they were uncomfortable. It occurred to me that this was, apparently, sometime after Constantine had declared Christianity the new state religion; however, I'm sure Roman soldiers, from time to time, helped themselves to a—shall we say—donation from the church to the supporting "protective" forces that kept them safe. Payoffs, extortion, and bribes are not an activity that originated in my current time; not all politicians and those hired to protect the citizens are reputable. Some, over the years, have been caught extorting and outright stealing from the population, while others have not.

One of the two priests hesitantly said, "We did not hear you come in. Is there something we can do for you?"

I am sure they expected us to stretch out our hand's palms up to receive a donation; they were visibly puzzled when Kolby asked, "What are your names, and what is this place?"

The shorter, wiry older priest said, "My name is Brother Johnathan, and my companion is Simeon. This is the meeting place for the new state religion called Christianity. How is it that you do not know this? You, after all, just entered from the outside."

"Yes, of course," Kolby said. "What I meant was, is this place where you are supposed to be doing this? It looks more like a place to store herbs than a treasury."

"Oh," said Brother Jonathan, "we had to hastily create an area inside the building to house our collections. We were not prepared for the tremendous influx of coins that have been offered recently. This room was not being used, so our leaders decided to utilize this as our treasury until the new larger facility could be erected.

What Is in a Name?

"So, your offerings have significantly increased as of late?" I inquired.

"Yes!" said Simeon, with a gleeful smile on his face, as he dropped a few coins on the small table in front of him. "No longer can we say, 'Silver and Gold have we none!'" His expression spoke volumes about his joy at the overflowing financial blessing the church was receiving.

The older Johnathan muttered, "Nor can we say 'Rise up and walk'" A frown of discontent flowed over his wrinkled face. "I would prefer to return to the days of no finances and the power of God rather than this new day of money and no power."

"Oh, you are so old fashion," the much younger Simeon said, "God does not work today as He did in the past. All of that miracle stuff is no longer needed. We are establishing the doctrinal truths that will assist us in spreading the Gospel, the government is on our side now, and things are changing."

"Gospel," Johnathan snapped. "A watered-down story if you ask me. When I was younger, we expounded on the ability and power of God to save people from sin and change their hearts. Nowadays, all you hear is, 'It is all about our *fidem* to God.' I don't know why they had to get rid of the old Greek word; I liked it much better. It had a mysterious element that is missing from our current word."

"You know the decision was made to abandon those

old Greek words for something newer, fresher, and more in tune with the language of the day. Latin is the new acceptable language of the people and much easier for them to understand without all the teaching about that antiquated Greek language. None of us younger people use it." Simeon spouted back like an unruly teenager.

Johnathan shot back with, "You say God doesn't do the miracle stuff anymore. Do you think He did those things to impress us? The problem isn't God. It is us; we have lost something!"

At that, I chimed in, "*Fidem* is the Latin word meaning fidelity or committed, confidence, belief, and trust. Why should that be of great concern? Isn't that what the old Greek word meant?"

"Exactly my point," Simeon said with a smug, I-told-you-so look on his face, "As I said, us younger people prefer the Latin to that old worn-out Greek language." He gave us a wink as if, since we were younger, we understood.

"No," Johnathan argued, "the Latin word lacks that something special; it is slightly off from the Greek word *pistis*. *Fidem* lacks one element that gave our preaching power and made our speech the Gospel. This younger generation has its doctrine, but the old ones had power and experience that is lacking today. Our Gospel has been reduced in one measure to a form of powerless religion."

"Powerless? How can you say powerless? Look at how

What Is in a Name?

many people are turning to Christ and making their decision to follow Him. Our meetings are so well attended that we barely have places for our high-ranking officials to sit. You know, we moved the common people out into the street and opened the windows so they could hear the message of the day," Simeon proudly countered.

"In the old days, there was no difference between people. Officials sat next to the pauper; the sick were brought before the old ones to lay hands on them and be healed. Today those who are beggars, unbelievers, and the sick are forced from our midst because they 'repulse' the officials and well-to-do. We are heading down a path from which I am not sure there is any return. Already we cannot say rise and walk. How much longer before we can no longer say Jesus saves? The winds of change are already laying the burden of salvation on our decision and our faithfulness to God." Johnathan was distraught as he mourned the loss of the old days.

Simeon simply rolled his eyes and touted, "You are stuck in the old days, wake up and join the new generation, brother."

I couldn't contain myself any longer. "Johnathan," I broke in, "that Greek word, *pistis*, you say the new word *fidem'* is missing an element; what is the element that is missing?"

Johnathan looked at me intently as if to see if I was

genuinely inquiring or poking fun at him. Once he was convinced I was serious, he said, "My child, I cannot tell you the answer; you must find it yourself. It will require you to travel back further than you already have. Go now, quickly to that place long ago, to the old ones, and they will help you find the piece missing from your shield." At that, a smile streamed across his face, and his eyes began to shimmer like that of an angelic being. He continued, "My heart is content to know that those of future days will seek the old ways. I can now rest knowing all is not lost, but one day the power will be restored."

Simeon looked at him with a deer-in-the-headlights look, astonished at his words.

Kolby and I were just as baffled by the old priest's knowledge of who we were and where we came from. I looked at Johnathan and said, "How do you know?"

"Kayla visited me yesterday and informed me of your arrival. I wasn't sure it was you until I saw your shield with the missing piece. Your journey is not over; you must continue. Remember this: There is more in a name than you might think!"

With that, our environment changed. We were still in Roman soldier attire, but the date was older, and something was different.

I glanced at Kolby; his face showed a puzzled look. I said, "What's wrong, Kolby?"

What Is in a Name?

He said, "I am amazed, I'm sure you don't know her, but Johnathan mentioned Kayla, a woman named Kayla is my friend in my time. It is strange that he should have a person in his time with the same name as the woman in my time and that the Kayla of his time should know of you and your quest."

"Wait a minute," I said, "You know a Kayla in your time?"

"Of course," Kolby said, "Kayla is a teacher of women in my time. She is well-known by all the Templars. She has a reputation as a female version of the Knights Templar. Her exploits are legendary. It is her teaching that stirred up my discontent."

"I thought you weren't supposed to have contact with women. How is it that Kayla has taught you?" I demanded.

Kolby defended his actions with, "Kayla is unusual; she has the ability to appear without notice. Her ability to enter a room without discovery far exceeds my abilities, and she is an incredible young woman with powers like no one I have ever met."

"Wait, you say she is a young woman?" I opened my mouth, and the words tumbled from my lips. What was Kayla? In my time, she was an old woman; in Kolby's, a young woman; and yet she appeared to Johnathan 900 years before Kolby was born and informed him that I would be coming. I couldn't take it any longer. I let go of the shield, and once again, I was in the Second Chance shop in Chicago, Illinois.

As my environment changed, I saw Kayla sitting in her chair, fumbling with something in her hand. There sat the old woman Kayla humming a tune that sounded more like an ancient Jewish melody than something from modern times.

"Who are you?" I blurted out, almost demanding. That was not how I meant it to sound; I was afraid, not angry.

This entire day, or was it several days? I wasn't sure how long I had either been gone or been in the shop. Time travel really messes with your mind. I've never really thought about time, but it appears it is not real; it is only human's way of understanding their lives. When I know how many twenty-four-hour days have passed, it provides me with a false sense of security. It is as if we are scratching a mark on the wall stating, "I was here." Without the measurement of time, we seem to lose something of our identity. Medical records, events, and all manner of things are connected to dates; without them, things seem to blur. However, that really doesn't change things, does it? Everything is relative; if we were eternal, which may be the case, not with our current bodies, but our conscious self, then the time spent in the mortal is but a blink of an eye in comparison to how long we will dwell in some other realm.

So, few of us think along these lines. Instead, we spend

What Is in a Name?

what time we have on earth piling up things that, in the grand scheme of things, really do not matter. We take more care primping in the morning before we face our world than we do preparing ourselves for the long term. My grandfather used to say, "The things that matter most, we focus on the least. Youth waste their energy chasing what cannot be gained, middle age wastes their energy trying to hang on to those things it never really had, and the aged seem to waste their energy fretting over what never was." Finding a balance in life requires an anchor or foundation that will never pass away. Grandfather would always say, "Build on a solid foundation, and your house will stand forever!" I never understood what he meant until these events began to unfold. Now after meeting Nya, Hynlee, Zachery, Kolby, Johnathan, and Kayla, I am beginning to realize that there is something or someone out there that is constantly trying to get us to surrender to a thing that is not real, rather than seeking those things that are real. Those things that are real are housed in a place that cannot be destroyed.

Kayla's response snapped me back to reality. "I am Kayla," she said calmly. "Have you forgotten so quickly?"

"That isn't what I meant, Kayla. You appear to me as an old woman, to Kolby in the 1200s as a young woman of great power and wisdom. You know a priest from the 1500s and one from somewhere around the year 300; how is that possible?" I was almost in tears; this entire experience was so far from my comfort zone I was shaken to my depths.

Kayla patted my hand with a motherly affection; her voice seemed to calm my anxiety. "My dear," she said in a low soothing voice, "have you not noticed that time is not real? We, you and I, have been granted the gift of understanding; that gift transcends man-made time. The secrets of the universe are at your disposal. You need only ask, and a way will be shown to you; seek the way with all your heart, and you will find a door, knock on that door, and it will be open to you. I told you I would never leave you; I would always be by your side; your journey is not complete, and to reduce the energy spent muddling through things, I have assisted you when I felt you needed it."

"You mean these events are real? This is not simply something rolling around in my head?" I was still having problems understanding what was going on.

"Of course, they are real, and yes, they are in your head. Your subconscious is active right now; your short breaks back into my little shop, into the conscious realm to ask me questions, allow the conscious mind a chance to wake up and ask what the subconscious is puzzled about." Kayla's words provided some clarification but did not answer my question about the reality of this, nor did they explain who she was, or did they?

"You will soon find," Kayla continued, "that the things the conscious mind is able to comprehend tend to be too slow for the subconscious, so the subconscious leaps to various places through a field of energy that eliminates

What Is in a Name?

seconds, minutes, hours, and days. You have been freed to wander the universe without the restraints of time. Very few have been able, without many years of dedicated focus, to reach the place you are now at. Even when the trained people reach a level that allows some of what you have experienced, very few can gain knowledge and understanding from those visits. You are special, Brea; you have a gift, use it to discover and assist, and it will continue to serve you and those around you who are seeking truth."

I was amazed at Kayla's answer. I had a gift. The ability to travel the universe and discover truths. I never knew a person could have this ability. What else are we, as humans, capable of? Then, I recalled a verse from the Bible, Paul the Apostle, in 2 Corinthians 12:2 (NRSV) said, "I know a person in Christ who fourteen years ago was caught up to the third heaven—whether in the body or out of the body I do not know; God knows." No wonder I was confused. It appears he was, too; at least for now, I could take comfort in thinking that he was.

Kayla smiled and suggested I get back to the business at hand; with that, I took hold of the shield and returned to my location with Kolby, who was standing exactly as he was when I left.

"Your disappearance amazes me, Brea," Kolby's wide-eyed gaze seemed almost boyish as he excitedly blurted out his amazement.

"How do you mean?" I asked as he stared. Admittedly, it made me a little uncomfortable.

"I know you are real, I held your hand, but I watched as you let go of the shield, and you seemed to fade as if a mist, and then you were gone. I was thinking about what Brother Johnathan said about the shield and all the talk about its name. When you met me, we talked about the new French/English word 'faith,' stemming from the French word that means fidelity or loyalty; that word replaced the Latin word for faith. Now we have discovered the Latin that was used for faith meant pretty much the same thing the English and French word meant. What does faith mean in your time, Brea?"

"I suppose, if you asked most people, it means trust and belief." I could see a pattern beginning to emerge even as I spoke the words. The English word "faith" in my time was only slightly different than the English/French word in Kolby's time, but it was different. In my time, our fidelity or loyalty was also dropped from the understanding of the word.

"It appears there is something in the name, the name on the shield, Brea. If you try to give the shield the name Faith, it won't fit; a part of it will still be missing. Most likely because the definition you give it is even less than those in my time give it, and ours slightly different than the Latin word, 900 years of separation from the original Greek word, and none, or at least few of us, know what is missing, or what it was that we gave up in the translation. *Pistis*, according to Brother Johnathan, may be the only name that will fit on that shield; if it does, then the name of the Shield Pistis means that it is the same name that Paul the Apostle gave it," Kolby said. He seemed to be constructing something in the air as he spoke, like placing pieces of a puzzle into their proper place.

"If you are right, Kolby," I was beginning to catch on to his train of thought, and almost simultaneously, we both said, "Ephesians 6:10–18, 'The armor of God, the shield!'"

"Of course, Kolby," I said as if I had known it all along.

Kolby rolled his eyes, knowing I was making fun of my own lack of understanding. "Brea," he continued, "you realize that if we are correct about this, when you return to your time, you will have the task of telling people about what we discover, don't you?"

His words nearly caused me to have a panic attack. Me challenging a concept that has been instilled in people for nearly 1700 years. I have a hard enough time trying to convince my hairstylist that my hairstyle is still in style when she wants to try something new. I could not imagine myself taking on the established teaching of my day with anything that would be contrary to what they and so many generations before them had been taught. Talk about taking on the establishment!

"I think we should press on Kolby and see why we are

where we are now," I said, hoping he wouldn't catch on to the fact that I was trying to change the subject.

With that suggestion, Kolby and I casually walked along the road we were on; as it circled a large mound of earth, it turned into an open field. The field was filled with all kinds of people, and they were obviously engaged in battle. Kolby did not hesitate to draw his sword from its sheath. He was ready to fight. I, on the other hand, was ready to run in the other direction. How could things have changed so rapidly? Then without notice, something nearly sliced my head off as it whizzed by my left ear. I turned and, perhaps with nothing more than sheer instinct, swung the shield around from its place on my back and took a hard blow to my shield, which nearly split in two. I fell to the ground, trembling and knowing that if I was struck again, I would certainly not survive.

Suddenly I heard a voice, a horrible voice that almost sounded like a slithering serpent voice. I couldn't believe my ears. "So you call yourself a Christian, don't you? You think you can take on hundreds of years of planting seeds and uproot what I have planted deep in tradition." Suddenly, something pierced my chest like a dart or an arrow, I tried to raise the shield to fend off a second arrow, but it pierced my shield as if my shield wasn't there; fortunately, it was deflected enough, and it only grazed my side. With that, the creature standing in front of me raised its bow once more, and the arrow released; it was heading right for my heart.

What Is in a Name?

At that moment, a sword blade struck the arrow and split it in two pieces, not vertically, but horizontally down the shaft of the arrow from the arrowhead, through the shaft, and out the fletching. The two halves of the arrow split around me and grazed both of my arms. Both arms immediately started burning like they were touched by a hot iron. Then I saw whatever it was that had spoken those words, it appeared like a mist, and it raised the sword held in its hand. The sword was going to score a direct hit, and I felt myself starting to fade into darkness. Suddenly I saw her, the warrior woman I saw the first night I touched the shield in Kayla's store. This woman was amazing; she stepped between me and the creature wielding the sword. The sword struck her shield with a sound that rumbled like thunder. The moment the sword hit the shield, the shield lit up with a bright white, a lightning white, and something like a sonic wave shattered the beast's sword, and fragments spewed out everywhere. With that, my defender swung her sword at the creature, and it immediately vaporized.

I thought to myself, *That sword, where have I seen it before?* Then I realized it was identical to the one that I saw the first night in the Second Chance store, but it was somehow different. I realized it was complete, that nothing was missing, and it was sharper than anything I had ever seen. The sword was also glowing like a white-hot flame, it sizzled, and sparks flew from it. Whoever this warrior woman was, she was amazing, accurate, and powerful. She raised the shield above me, and what seemed like a force field draped over me like a protective pod. As I lay there on the ground, the tears flowing from my eyes, my body wreathing in pain, I felt a deep ache in my heart; the first arrow had struck so deep I was sure it was going to end my life. I lifted my eyes up and gazed at the shield. When it was protecting me, it had been glowing; now, it was transparent, with one exception, the portion that had a word written on it. I could make out the word; it was Greek, only one word. Through my teary eyes, I could read it; as I spoke the word, something changed. The ache in my heart instantly disappeared, I looked down, and where blood had been pumping out of the wound with each heartbeat, there was now only a scar. That word had power like nothing I had ever experienced before, but the word wasn't mine. It was the warrior woman's, the name I had been searching for, the name that gave power to the shield, the woman who stood above me protecting me was in possession of a complete shield that had power. That word, what was it? I strained to read it, and then it became clear: *PISTIS*. I realized instantly that Kayla had been right. Whatever it was about, that name that provided power was worth discovering.

My eyes turned toward the woman holding the shield above me. Something about her was so familiar, yet different. I know this is going to sound weird; however, I was certain I wasn't wrong. It couldn't be, but it was; it had to be, I strained to see, and it was Kayla. The bands around her forearm were like the ones I caught a glimpse of on

What Is in a Name?

one of my returns to the Second Chance store. How is this possible? She is so young and powerful, not like the old woman Kayla I talk with in the store in my time.

Time, remember what Kayla said about time. It isn't real. Time is just a tool that humans use to create the illusion of stability and security in a temporal world, but that world may not be real; in fact, the Bible says it isn't.

I was about to speak, but Kayla spoke first. "I told you I would be with you every step of the way; do you believe that now?"

"Yes, I do, Kayla. You have proven to me that you are with me." This was probably the first time in my life, or at least in my remembrance, that I could honestly say I believed deep down inside.

Could I doubt? The woman had just saved my life. I repeated, "Of course, I believe; you just provided me with evidence to back up your words." There it was again, that word *evidence*, that part of the meaning of the name on the shield. I looked at my own shield, where the nameplate was filling in. I now saw a greater portion of it restored. The letters IST were clearly visible, and now the hole that was once in my shield was filling in even more.

With that thought, I turned toward Kayla and started to speak her name, "Kay—" That was as far as I got. She suddenly faded from the scene; in fact, the entire landscape changed; it was clear Kolby and I were no longer on a battlefield. We were in a pleasant little village somewhere in the Roman Empire, but time had changed; for some reason, I could sense it. We were in a time between 1 CE and 100 CE.

"Kolby," I said, "you fought valiantly during that battle. How is it that you were not struck down? I had no defense against that enemy, and yet you stood your ground."

Kolby looked at me with a comforting look and said, "Evidence, Brea, I have been in a great number of battles, and God always delivered me from them. I trust Him because He has proven Himself true to me. As a result of His past protection, I knew, in my heart, I would survive. You might call it a conviction. Besides, that enemy's arrows could not pierce my breastplate; the shield was useless, the arrows went right through it, but when they hit the breastplate, they bounced off like a child's toy arrow."

I looked at his breastplate. For the first time since Kolby and I met, I saw a name on it, one word in Latin: *LUSTITIA*. "Kolby," I asked, "what does that name on your breastplate signify?"

"I fight for righteousness; we, or at least I, as a Templar Knight, fight for righteousness; however, as I told you when we began this journey, I am disillusioned by the direction of the Templars. Something is missing; the sword is not as powerful as it once was, and the shield lacks something as well. When I first started with the Templars, I had the Latin word *Iustitia* meaning righteousness, imprinted on my breastplate to remind me of my mission, and my mission was not to conquer but rather do the right thing. I seek righteousness," Kolby said with a deep conviction.

"You certainly seem to believe what you are saying, Kolby. It appears you have deep convictions about this," I responded, and then the word *conviction* seemed to ring in my ears. Conviction... A deep conviction in a thing; that conviction is lacking in my life.

"It is part of who I am," Kolby reasoned. "to violate that conviction would be to die. I have given my life over to seeking what is right, and it is that quest that has caused me to doubt the organization to which I have committed myself. I cannot stay with a group or a community that does not share such a deep conviction for righteousness. It is a part of who I am."

Evidence restored part of the name on my shield. I wondered if *conviction* was part of the name as well. With that thought, I looked at my shield, and more of the word displayed and filled in the space previously open by the missing name ISTI was now exposed. I could clearly see what had been missing from our English word faith—it was the idea of *evidence* and *conviction*. But that made no sense. We had evidence in the testimony of others and the recorded words in the Bible, yet that didn't seem to be as powerful as the two pieces of evidence I had just witnessed that produced belief in me. Kayla provided personal evidence by protecting me, and Kolby's breastplate was evidence that his quest for righteousness would protect him from the arrows of the enemy. Could it be that personal evidence, I mean having something that is exclusively for me or specially designed for me, was required for faith to be whole or powerful enough to change my life? "Experiential evidence, current, not historic," I spoke it out loud, and it settled down deep in my chest. As it did, it seemed like a weight lifted off my heart. As I spoke those words, I looked at the shield, and again a change added to the letters ISTI, more of the open space filled in. My heart leaped inside my chest, and my mind seemed to be enlightened like never before. We were close to the end of this quest. I could sense it. But what was still missing?

I now understood that *evidence* and *conviction* were part of the definition that was long forgotten in my time. It was clear to me there is more to a name than just a name. There is a meaning, and that meaning can change everything. If you lose the meaning, you lose the name, and if you lose the name, you lose the power it produces. What's in a name? With that thought, I turned loose of the shield and returned to the Second Chance store and to Kayla.

CHAPTER 8

THE LAST SHALL BE FIRST

I didn't say a word; I simply hugged Kayla and wept. I had a friend who was closer to me than a sister, a sister who would not leave me, a sister who would protect me when I couldn't protect myself. Never in my life had I experienced such unmerited love and kindness. It seemed like several minutes before I could compose myself.

When I finally released her, something was different. The old woman Kayla suddenly was the young warrior woman Kayla, a huge smile stretched across her face, and she said, "I'm so proud of you, you have been so brave and determined, and your quest is nearly over. So, tell me what you have learned so far?"

I wanted to ask Kayla how she was able to alter her appearance, but something inside told me I already knew the answer. Her appearance hadn't changed; my vision of her had. "Evidence and conviction," I said. "Our current understanding defines faith as our belief and our trust, but clearly, evidence and conviction are a powerful part of faith. However, I'm confused, the name on the shield is nearly restored, yet the first and last letters are still missing and illusive."

"A very wise teacher once said, 'The first shall be last and the last first;' it would do you well to remember at least the first part of that as you seek the last letters of the name," Kayla responded.

"I find it odd that we, in our current world, have lost so much in the translation of the word faith. The Latin word seemed to have altered our understanding somewhat. That word *Fidem* appears to have obscured the idea of evidence and conviction, although it did imply something of that nature. Then the French and English words separated us even further from the original, so much so that we, in current times, see faith as something we do; no one seems to have any idea that things have changed. Traditional teaching, even when it is hundreds of years old, is still only tradition; truth, on the other hand, has always been and will always be." I said as I considered the departure from the truth, which started two-millennium before I was born.

"The enemy of truth seldom causes a huge disruption; that enemy is more cunning than that. A slight alteration here, a small diversion there, is all it takes, given enough retelling of the falsehood," Kayla said.

"I remember something from my grade school days about lines," I replied. "If you make a huge change in the direction of the line, it is immediately recognized, as in a 90-degree angle; however, if you are only a micrometer off, the shift would be barely noticeable unless given enough distance from the diversion. Traveling a block may not cause an issue; however, if your journey were a greater distance, let's say Mars, and you were off by that much, you would certainly miss the mark, if not miss the planet entirely. If our end game is heaven and we are following a path that was altered by only a small amount, we might miss it completely. I never realized how crucial it was to stay on track."

"Thank you so much, Kayla. I am returning with an increased sense of purpose and feel assured I will succeed knowing I am not alone." I said as I took hold of the shield again.

As I was making the transition, I heard Kayla's voice say, "The battle is not over until you win."

Those words concerned me; was I about to enter another battle? Then I realized it would be okay; Kolby was by my side fighting the righteous fight, and Kayla was with me and would not leave me. I believed that all would be alright.

When I returned, Kolby and I began to assess the situation and the town we were now walking through. Both of us heard a noise coming from what appeared to be a building slightly different than the small one-room dwellings we were walking by. The closer we drew to the building, the more we could hear. Inside, people were singing. The melody was consistent; however, the words were jumbled, as if everyone was singing their own song. We stepped up to the doorway and immediately, what seemed like confusion, aligned to produce a unified song of praise. It was so beautiful and heartfelt; it moved me deep inside my being. Something so pure and real about the words being sung, like a song I've never heard before.

I have been to a lot of church gatherings, and the words sung by the congregation typically follow a pattern set forth by the songwriter. This melody, however, was different. It still seemed like it was being followed like a normal song, but the words coming out of the mouth of the singers were each different, yet they flowed together, mingled, and produced an incredible message of love and praise. Their message blended like waters from several streams coming together, creating a larger river, each voice having its own origin, then suddenly coming together, joining forces, and becoming a powerful message, unified by the original fountain from which each flowed.

Kolby and I were deeply moved. I glanced at him, and his eyes were filled with tears, not of sorrow but joy. I felt my cheeks grow cold as my own tears flowed down my face, and with that, something deep down inside of me began to impact me. It was heaviness; it was so concentrated it felt like a bag of rocks sitting on top of my heart and lungs, making it difficult to breathe. Like an out-of-body experience, my spirit seemed to separate from my body. As I gazed at what appeared to be me, or at least the physical me, I saw a pouch like the one in the Second Chance store, the one Kayla brought out to me that first night in the shop. It began to lift off my chest. As it did, I saw writing on it, I strained to see what it was, and then the word jumped off the bag in 3D, Brea Rea Joyce. With that, the weight on my heart and lungs lifted. The strings on the bag began to loosen, and words began to float out of it. Words like, hurt, pain, lies, and betrayal. With each word that lifted, it was trailed by images of times in my life when each of these things had impacted me and produced my broken believer. I felt a joy beginning to well up within me, a joy I could not verbalize; I could only enjoy and surrender to it. Then suddenly, as quickly as it started, everything drew back into the bag; the string pulled tight and sunk back into my heart and lungs like a huge rock.

The room that had been filled with people singing the beautiful song of praise and love dissolved and melded into the battlefield once again. My heart sank, and my hope flew from me like a rocket shot across the landscape. The tears of joy, which were flowing down my cheeks, turned to red hot trails of lava burning away everything that was happy in my life. Then I heard it again, that voice, the one from my previous battle. I was horrified. I knew what was about to happen.

The battlefield smelled of rotting corpses, blood mingled

with dirt, and people from all walks of life. This was it, and this was the horrible, terrifying scene from my first night in Kayla's shop. Where was she? Where was Kolby? My vision was hampered by something pouring down my face over my eyes. I reached up with my right hand and rubbed it across my face; as I pulled back, I saw blood, my blood. I suspected I must have a head wound. Again, I felt the life beginning to drain from my body. Then there was that voice; it sounded like thunder booming in my ears, yet not my ears; it was a voice shouting from within.

Suddenly, I recognized that voice; it was the same voice I had heard for years, telling me I could not do it. Do what? It really didn't matter; it was the voice I had to overcome so many times, a voice that represented success and failure. When I felt strongly about a thing and forced that voice out of my head and heart, I would reach up and find some success, but never complete success. Even when I succeeded, it seemed to steal my joy, like a virus sapping my strength. I realized, at that moment, I never felt healthy; I always felt incomplete. When I graduated from high school, I was elated, having accomplished something that no one in my family had ever done. That joy was mingled with a feeling of worthlessness; that feeling came from this voice speaking inside of me. When I entered college, that voice kept haunting me, telling me I wouldn't succeed. When I graduated from college, it told me I wouldn't succeed in the career I chose. I fought it all the time. I suddenly felt so tired and tired of fighting something I could not seem to be rid of.

At some point in my life, I determined I was destined to fight this inner failure voice forever. On this battlefield, all the years and energy fighting this feeling of worthlessness weighed on me like a ton of bricks, and I sank to the ground under the weight. Then I saw it again, the pouch, or bag, or whatever it was. It was sitting outside of my body on my chest, crushing me to the ground. I could read my name on it, Brea Rea Joyce. At that moment, it dawned on me I had just learned there was something in a name; my name, Brea Rea Joyce. What was in that name? Why was it suddenly haunting me as if I was failing to fulfill some predetermined destiny that sprung up from the name given to me when I was born? A stupid name, a name that got me teased in school, that was the basis of jokes in college, and that was scorned when I attended churches and was not happy. Those places always seemed to make me sad. At that moment, deep in my heart, I even suspected my parents of making fun of me by labeling me with my name. Everything about me screamed worthless, a joke, a mess, unloved, unwanted, a person who ruined everyone and everything I encountered.

Deep in thought and oblivious to what was happening around me, I was suddenly aware of a presence beside me. Out of the corner of my left eye, I saw the flash of a sword aiming right for my worthless shield; however, the moment it struck the shield, it was deflected by another sword that I realized was Kayla's. She was there, right at my side, just as she promised. Her protection as my friend and, in some deep way, my sister was comforting, but that was short-lived. Suddenly, out of the corner of my blood-soaked eye, I saw an arrow, more like a dart; it was too close for Kayla to respond to. In fact, she didn't even try. I thought to myself, *Please, Kayla, don't be like all the rest who have left me in my deepest moment of need.* "Please protect me. Please, help," I cried.

In an instant, the arrow struck my right eye. It hurt slightly, but I knew I was done for. Then something strange occurred: The arrow, instead of piercing my eye, bounced off and fell to the ground. *What just happened?* I thought to myself. That arrow hit its mark, and yet it did not pierce me. I looked up, and Kayla was standing over me with a smile on her face. Then I caught a glimpse of Kolby on my right, standing there, allowing the arrows to bounce off his breastplate. He, too, was smiling and swinging the sword that was in his hand. That sword, his sword, different now, gleaming like Kayla's sword, sharp, sharper than anything I had ever seen. Something changed; something happened. Where did he get this new sword? We were together in that place where everyone was singing. He never left; we went right from there to this battlefield. When did his sword change, and why? I lifted my head, and all around this battlefield, I saw them; the people in my first vision of this scene, people from different time periods and various backgrounds; people of different colors, sizes, and stations in life; people from all over the world fighting the vapor

The Last Shall Be First

enemy; some successful some not.

Two people on the field right in front of me were drenched in blood; I was horrified by the scene and yet could not look away. As I gazed at them, for the first time, I saw the strangest thing, arrows bouncing off them; were these people made of steel or something? Not one of the arrows pierced these two people. The arrows were flying at them as if they were being launched from a rapid-fire automatic weapon, and yet not one of them penetrated. How could that be? Then, I realized the blood they were covered with was not their own; in fact, each of them had a person that appeared like Kayla standing on their left side, pouring the blood over them. There on their right side was another like Kolby standing on their right, allowing the arrows to bounce off their breastplate.

That blood, what was it? The way they were pouring it out seemed like they were not concerned about it running out. That cup they held in their hand looked like something from a dinner table in Jesus' time. That being the case, it would sooner or later run out, cups are not continuously full, and yet the blood did not slow; it increased. As it did, the protective coating over each of the people in front of me increased, and I became more resistant to the arrows of the enemy. The people in front of me began to rise from their knees, and as they did, their physiques began to change; they were no longer weak and helpless. They were beginning to look like bodybuilders or something. One of the two was a man dressed in a business suit, yet he appeared to be, some type of gangster or something; the other was a woman whose profession was probably one of the oldest in the world.

Then I saw more people like them, with someone on their right and another on their left, everyone was doing the same thing, and the result was the same. *Everyone except me*, I thought, "Here we go again; everyone gets it but me!"

As quickly as this scene had appeared, it changed. Kayla and Kolby were gone. I was alone in a room, and in front of me was a man, an old man, a man who smelt like sweat and garlic; his complexion was a darker color, and I realized he was Jewish. I was sitting on the floor with a table in between us; he was reaching across the table, offering me something to eat and drink.

I shook my head from side to side, trying to regain both my vision and sense of where I was and what was going on. "Who… Who are you?" I asked, not sure I wanted to know.

"My name is Thomas." He said in a fatherly sort of way. "What can I do for you?"

"Aren't you the least bit confused by my appearance here at your table?" I asked.

"Of course not, Brea. I was made aware of your quest several days ago and was instructed to prepare a meal for you that was fit for a queen. Please nourish yourself; you must be famished after all your travels. Please tell me how is Kayla and her friend Kolby. Is Zachary in good health?"

I was speechless; I shook my head again and said, "Who are you people, and what is going on?"

Thomas set a bowl in front of me; it was filled with a kind of stew or something; it smelled very tasty. I picked up the utensil next to me and took a taste. It was delicious. Next to the bowl was a small loaf of bread. I picked it up, broke it, and tasted it. It was sweet tasting, and yet it reminded me of the warm bread my grandmother used to make when we would go to her house for visits. There, in front of me, was a cup filled with what appeared to be wine. I lifted it to my lips, took a sip, and realized it was water, cool cold water, but why did it look like wine? "This is so refreshing," I said to Thomas. "What is it?"

"It is the water from the well that never runs dry," he replied. "It gives life to all who will drink of the cup."

"I see," I muttered in a voice with an enunciation that was sarcastic.

Thomas ignored my unbelief and continued, "I would like to tell you a story if you are willing to listen."

"You are my host, I am your guest, and it would be rude to refuse. Please tell me your story." I said, a bit embarrassed by my own rudeness to my host.

"A very long time ago, or was it just yesterday? Time, what a fickle thing man has conjured up. Some friends of mine made a claim that was most disturbing, and I refused to believe them without the most credible proof. They could have made fun of me and called me a doubter. I didn't care; I was honest with them, and even at the point of possibly being cast off by them, I was willing to stand my ground. Can you identify with me, Brea?"

"Absolutely," I said. "This was the reason for my quest. I can't seem to believe; I keep telling people my believer is broken. They keep saying, 'Just believe,' and I keep telling them I can't. They don't understand, I need proof, and none of them seem able to offer it to me. It isn't like I refuse to believe; I just can't. Every time I make a commitment to believe a thing, within a few hours or at most a day or two, that belief dissolves, and I'm left broken."

"You need evidence, something that is so clear it is unmistakable." Thomas said, "Once you have it, provided it is from a credible source, it produces a conviction deep within you, and nothing and no one can alter that conviction. On that conviction, you will live or die. Am I correct in my evaluation of you?"

I looked at Thomas; tears began to fill in my eyes. How could this man, whom I just met, know me so deeply? "Yes!" I sighed. "How did you know?"

"Because, Brea, I am Thomas. You might know me better by the fact that I am the other or the twin. Over time, tradition has declared me 'Doubting Thomas.'"

I was stunned; could this be the Thomas of the Bible, the guy who refused to believe unless he put his fingers in the holes in Christ's hands and his hand in the hole in his side? "Are... Are you the Apostle Thomas?" I was sure he would laugh at me; instead, his words came out comforting and full of wisdom.

"Brea," he said, "I could have very easily agreed with my companions and said I believed; however, in my heart, I would have known it to be a lie. If my reason for saying I believed something I did not believe was to appease my companions, my friends, the men whom I had traveled and lived with for three years, I would have been worse than a liar. By saying what I did, I exposed myself to ridicule. However, God knows our hearts, each of us is like the soil in the ground, some soft and pliable, and some hard as a rock as the result of things in our lives. I was always Thomas, the twin; I lost my identity to history, so much so that today, in your time, no one knows my real name, and if I was a twin, no one knows who my brother might have been. Should I disclose this to you now? Shall I tell you my real name? What would be the point? Who would believe you? So let it suffice to say I am Doubting Thomas. If you think about it, Brea, I am a twin to everyone who, like you, doubts and does not find within them the ability to believe."

Thomas' words were like a quenching drink to my thirsty soul. To think another, one whom history portrays as the doubter, would have had the courage to stand up to his friends and declare what was truly in his heart. It would have been easy for him to hide his doubt and join in with those who proclaimed the message of the risen Jesus. But he did not; he stood fast. I suddenly felt like Thomas and I were cut from the same mold, I was not the only person in history who could not believe what they were told, and I was not the only person that needed proof.

Thomas continued, "Brea, do you know what I was lacking that prevented me from believing what the others were telling me?"

"The ability to believe," I responded, unsure if that was the answer. It was simply what I felt.

"No, Brea, the ability to believe was not the thing I lacked. All traditional historical teachings miss this very important truth; traditional history is so busy putting me down for not believing they completely miss the Hebrew meaning of faith. You see, *Emunah* (Hebrew) stems from a root that indicates fidelity. To understand the power of that word, you must realize that throughout the Torah, we, who are Jews, were called on to remember God's faithfulness. What most fail to realize is that without prior experience, it is impossible to remember. Somewhere in a person's past, they must have had an experience to remember." Thomas seemed to be trying to get me to see something that I apparently was not seeing.

At that point, Thomas said, "Brea, what did the other disciples have that I did not? Think before you speak, what were they in possession of that I was not a part of?"

"Well," I started slowly, "they had each other to support their claim, and each of them believed that Jesus had risen."

"And why did they believe that He had risen?" Thomas was nudging me closer to where he needed me to be. I could tell from the gleam in his eye.

"They had seen him, and you had not?" The light finally went on in my head. Evidence and conviction, the two points of faith I discovered that were missing from my current understanding of Faith. I continued, "Jesus had shown himself to them; however, you were not there. They believed because they had seen him, you had not, and yet they were trying to get you to believe based on their evidence, but you couldn't because something like that, something so far outside the ability of any human to believe, has got to have an undeniable proof before a person can genuinely believe. That individual must experience for themselves; they cannot live on the experience of another."

"And who provided them with that evidence, Brea?" Thomas pushed me a little further, and I was about to open my eyes.

"Jesus!" I declared, and with that, I fully expected the shield in my hand to be complete. I looked at it, and still, no P finishing the word PISTIS, but the letter S was displayed. The name on the shield was still incomplete. What was it that I was not seeing?

Then Thomas said, "Who was Jesus?"

"The Messiah," I said, rather reluctant. I was still not understanding.

"Brea, the Messiah, the Son of God, taking what is God's and making it known unto us. He was God among us. What He revealed was the same as God revealing it. Do you understand?"

"Yes, but no, I do not think I understand what you are trying to get me to see." I felt frustrated by this conversation.

It was at that point that Thomas put his hand on my shoulder, smiled, and said, "Let me help you, my precious child. The word you are looking for, the name on your shield, PISTIS; your generation uses the word Faith. In the first-century Greek language, the word means evidence and conviction. If you follow this through, you begin to understand that it is not only the evidence that brings conviction; it is the source of that evidence. You see, Peter and the others were not Jesus, and they were not God. Men will deceive; God cannot. God cannot lie; therefore, whatever He says is and always will be. His words endure forever; they never change. His word creates what was not simply by speaking it."

Thomas's face turned solemn, and his voice soft yet stern as he continued, "The matter at hand has to do with eternity. Should you, or anyone, put the hope of the salvation of their soul, their eternal destiny, in the hands of mere men and women? This matter has to do with a realm that God oversees, not man. When you die, Peter, James, or John will not welcome you into God's Kingdom, God Himself is the ruler; He alone can say who will and who won't enter. When you stand before Him, will you use as your defense the fact that you believed a certain human or a certain teaching and, therefore, you should be allowed into His Kingdom? He will scoff at you and say, 'Depart from me; I never knew you.' The evidence required must come from God himself, and that alone can produce in you the conviction that changes. *Divine evidence and conviction,* Brea, is the only thing that can change the heart. God Himself proving the thing to you! You need the word of God; on that word alone, you can stand."

"Divine evidence and conviction, the word of God; are you telling me I have to believe the Bible?" I responded.

"Brea, Jehovah is alive. We who are mortal on this earth can give testimony to what we have seen and heard; however, like Peter and the others, we do not have the power, in and of ourselves, to enable evidence and conviction. We can lead you to Him and provide you with our testimony, the Bible you read, the written record, at least in part, of all that God has done among us. The purpose of the collection of books you call the Bible is intended to explain and lead you to God, not to replace Him or your need to have a personal relationship with Him. The mystery of that relationship eludes the religious; it is those who are brought to life in spirit that are anchored because of it. If you understood the Bible, you would see it points you to that place where you meet God. When the recorded words become a substitute for the living word, religion is all you have. We, on the other hand, are spiritual, not religious. Nothing short of God speaking to our hearts can suffice. Brother Paul declared what the prophets of old cried out; the message they shared is that we are not simply sick in our natural selves; we are indeed dead. Dead like Lazarus and only the power of God speaking to us can produce life in us and what is needed to sustain that life. Life, Brea, spiritual life is the gift of God; Jehovah is in the business of speaking things into existence that previously were not. We, who were dead, are now alive because He spoke life into us. Go back and read the creation story, and you will see that moment when mankind became a living soul," Thomas said with deep conviction and clear understanding.

Thomas spoke with such power and deep conviction that it moved something deep within me. I was shocked and said, "But that would mean that God has got to communicate with me directly. Are you telling me that without God speaking to my heart, I cannot possibly believe? That without God-provided evidence, any commitment I make to a manmade idea is not real faith?"

Thomas replied, "Brother Paul wrote to the church at Rome and said much about all of this; let me sum it up for you. When we were still sinners, godless, powerless, Christ died for us. God initiated the cure. If any of this depends on you, then it is by works, not grace, that you are saved. If you are saved because you have arrived at a point of belief or decided to believe without any direct activity from God, then you are the author of your own salvation."

Thomas continued, "This life we now live is the result of God's ongoing activity in our life. There is a group that is starting to gain some traction among us. They believe in God. However, their idea of God is that He started this at the beginning and will catch it at the end, but what happens in between, God is not involved in. Nothing could be further from the truth; you must understand that if it were not for His nudging us, none of us would have one thought about Him. Remember, Paul said, while we were powerless and godless, these are not just words; they are reality. To suspect anything different is to deny the truth that all of us were dead in our trespasses and sins. To suppose that any of us can have one spiritual thought without the prompting of God is to declare all of Scripture as a lie."

I suddenly recalled something an old minister once told me. He said there are a couple of ways to look at this. One is the way a Deist views life; they believe exactly as Thomas had just said; God started it and will finish it but does not involve Himself daily. The other view is that of a Theist; a Theist believes that God started it all and continues to be actively involved moment by moment in the creation as it travels to the end and to His purpose. The old minister said, "I am a Theist, and I am not alone. God is with me each moment; all my thoughts about Him are the result of His prompting, and none of this is my doing. It is all about

Him."

As I considered Thomas's words, I remembered what Kayla had said to me: "The last first." The last thing I learned is that PISTIS begins with the Divine, not evidence. It is evidence provided to us by God; it flows from Him. If any of us believes—and I mean truly believes—it is because He has provided the evidence that enables us to believe. So, the last was indeed the first. I looked at the shield, and there, in front of me, was what appeared to be a complete shield lacking nothing. The word PISTIS was complete. With that, I was sure my quest was over. I did it, I discovered all the missing pieces, and the shield was now whole.

I thanked Thomas for all his wisdom and for allowing me to finally understand. I smiled and hugged the old man and said, "From this point going forward, I will no longer call you Doubting Thomas, but rather Honest Thomas. Your reputation has been tarnished by those who failed to see what was really going on. Peter and all the rest should have known better."

With that, Thomas said, "Brea, what makes you think Peter and my other companions scoffed at me and called me Doubter? Tradition, my child, can pervert even the most profound truth, given enough time. Understand; this is not the end of your journey. To know the things you know is not enough. Remember, He must provide the evidence you need. I said to the other Apostles, 'Unless I put my fingers in the holes in his hand, and my hand in his side, I will not believe. When all was said and done, it did not take that Jesus would have given me exactly what I asked, but when it came down to it, I did not need to touch; I simply needed to see Him. His words still ring in my ears, 'Because you have seen me, you have believed; blessed are those who have not seen and yet have believed' (John 20:29, NIV). What you seek is still ahead of you; brace for impact."

Instantly I was back on the battlefield, blow after blow struck the shield, but it did not fail me this time; it was whole. However, I was not. I remember at that moment, I cried out, "Help me believe; I must believe."

Then, I realized I could bring the battle to an end by simply letting go of the shield. With that thought, I released and was instantly standing in the Second Chance shop with Kayla. Kayla had resumed her old woman disguise; I was puzzled by her aged appearance and asked, "Why did you return as an old woman again?"

"Age, my dear, can, in many cases, cause people to view a person differently than they otherwise would. For example, when you look at me like this, do you see power or wisdom? Are you more relaxed sharing with an old woman or a young, powerful warrior? Besides, it is comfortable, much like a well-worn pair of slippers." Kayla said as she tugged at some of the loose-fitting skin around her sagging jowls.

At that, I had to laugh and responded, "I see what you mean; I probably would not have returned after that first night if I had seen you in your battle gear."

"Tell me, Brea, what have you learned? I see the nameplate is nearly complete; PISTIS has been restored." Kayla pointed at the nameplate on the shield as she spoke.

It was then I realized there were still two small holes in the shield; something was still missing, but what was it? "I learned the complete meaning of the word Pistis; it is Divine Evidence and Conviction. You were right, the last thing I learned was the first part of the meaning, and it begins with God. I don't understand why the shield is not whole. I know the definition of the word, and the word *Pistis* has been restored to the shield. What am I missing?" My response was one of exhaustion and frustration. I had endured several battles, some had left me wounded deep inside, and the thought of returning to that battlefield created something more than fear. I was running out of energy; I couldn't survive another one of those battles. If I had time to examine myself, I would most likely declare I was at the end of it all. I had nothing left to give; I had reached the end of me.

Kayla must have sensed my hesitation. Her words encouraged, "Brea, when we get to the end of our own strength, that is when the supernatural strength must persevere. At this point, if you return—and returning is entirely up to you—there is a chance you might not survive.

The Last Shall Be First

The question at hand is simple; how badly do you want this thing you are seeking?"

"I must have it!" I responded. "Right now, at this moment, I want nothing else. It is as important to me as breathing. Without it, I will not survive. I do not want to travel another step. I must have this problem of a broken believer fixed now. I am hungry for this truth. I am as thirsty as I would be crossing a one-hundred-mile desert in the heat of the day on foot."

"Then it is settled; you must return and finish your quest." As Kayla spoke those words, a look of satisfaction crossed her face. I wasn't sure what was about to happen, but if it meant the end of my life, it didn't matter; I would not be denied.

"What I don't understand is how I get the evidence I need to complete this. Obviously, it could come from the Bible, but reading that, while interesting, has never produced in me what Thomas seemed to be telling me we all need. The testimony of friends is not sufficient, that Thomas made abundantly clear, so what is it, and how do I get it?" I asked.

Kayla motioned to the shield and said, "Your answer is not here. It is there; if you want to find what you are looking for, you must go back."

With that, I took hold of the shield once more, and instantly, I was back in first-century Rome. The battlefield was gone, and Kolby and I were standing on the street of what seemed to be Jerusalem. I turned to him and said, "Kolby, have you found what you were looking for yet?"

"To some extent, yes," Kolby's expression told me he was as confused by all of this as I was. His sword was complete, but it was not as sharp as it appeared in my last battle. "Something is still not right, Brea. The sword is complete but not very sharp. It is like a body with no life."

"But, Kolby," I responded, "I saw the sword in that last battle. The sword in your hand was glowing and sharper than anything I have ever seen. What happened?"

"I don't know," Kolby said as he looked over the sword. "One moment, the sword appeared on fire; the next, it was as lifeless as you see it now."

"It would appear neither of us has completely discovered the thing we are looking for," I said, trying to hold back my disappointment and fatigue. "I sincerely hoped you, at least, had discovered what was missing in your life. Your sword and my shield are both complete, but they lack the power to perform. What are we missing, and why can't we seem to find it?"

CHAPTER 9
THE WORD OF GOD

As we walked by one of the dwellings, the door opened, and a young man stepped out into the street; he turned, looked both ways and spotted us. Without saying a word, he motioned to us to enter his dwelling. I thought, *This is very odd; we are in Roman soldier attire, and yet this man is inviting us in; this is not typical for this time in history when most despise and fear the Roman soldiers. How is it that he is inviting us in?*

Kolby and I entered the dwelling and discovered we were not alone with the young man. There were several people sitting around a table enjoying a meal. The young man was the first to speak. "Greetings, fellow traveler; my name is Nolan. These are my two companions, Talya and Saylor. We are keepers of the word!"

I am not sure why either of us was surprised by Nolan's knowledge of who we were; it seemed like the norm in this quest. How did all these people know who we were and who prepared them for our arrival?

"Nice to meet you, Nolan. What do you mean keepers of the word?" Kolby asked.

"It is our calling to preserve all the words our teachers have shared with us. We are writing most of them down. This meeting is our group, and we help ensure that stories and teachings are accurate. We believe these things are important to the future, and we want to make sure they are as close as possible to what was originally said by the Apostles and our Lord. If we delay any longer, things tend to get lost to tradition; therefore, recording them is the best way to avoid error," Nolan explained.

"For the word of God is alive and active. Sharper than any double-edged sword, it penetrates even to dividing soul and spirit, joints, and marrow; it judges the thoughts and attitudes of the heart" (Hebrews 4:12, NIV). Kolby responded, "You are in possession of such a word?"

Nolan laughed and said, "You sound like Brother Paul; he talks like that. No, Kolby, we are in possession of the recorded and shared words spoken by men who were and are inspired by God. What you speak of is in the past, present, and future."

"I don't understand," Kolby said, puzzled, "what do you mean it is in the past, in the present, and in the future? Everything that God spoke is in the past, not the present or future. By the way, what is the year?"

"It has been fifty years since the resurrection," Nolan replied. "Why do you think the living God only spoke in the past? You appear to be of that belief some are beginning to hold to, that God is not concerned about our daily lives, only His end plan. He has spoken to all of us, including you and Brea."

At that, Talya spoke up, "Are you not aware of the teachings of the ancients about *Pistis*?"

"Why do you think you are here?" Saylor asked.

At that, I joined the conversation. "I'm searching for the ability to believe. Kolby is seeking the power of the word. Apparently, both were lost to tradition somewhere from this time to ours."

"Is our labor in vain?" Nolan asked.

"Apparently not," I responded. "If it were, we would not be here, something of your work has endured throughout the centuries, or no one in my time would be seeking anything, and yet here I am. Also, I'm curious, how did you know we were coming, and how did you know when to look for us?"

Talya was quick to respond, "During our meditation, we were instructed by a voice speaking to us. Each of us heard it clearly. We recognized it as the voice of our Lord. He shared all that we needed to know about…you, your, um, er, your names, your in…in…individual quest, and at the right moment, He told Nolan to step outside and invite you in." Talya was bouncing with excitement and could hardly keep the words straight.

I was stunned. "Your Lord spoke to you about us?" I said in disbelief, and yet the fact that they knew about us was proof they were telling the truth. "How did He..." I stopped midsentence; I suddenly became increasingly aware of my unbelief. I suddenly realized that deep in my being, that core that dictates our actions and lives, the place the Bible calls the heart, *I did not believe that God or Jesus was real.*

Saylor took my hand and pressed it warmly between her two hands, smiled a soft smile, and said, "It is okay, Brea; each of us had to come to this point in our lives before God was able to do something with us. If we think we believe, without the word spoken to our hearts, He cannot help us. It is only when we realize and acknowledge our unbelief and our inability to believe without His help that we have arrived at the point of enlightenment."

I collapsed to the floor. The weight of that thing in my heart was more than I could take. My eyes filled with tears, and my heart was breaking. All these years, I said I believed in God, I sought Him, and admitted I didn't believe God saved me. All the while I was saying I couldn't believe, I was acting like I did at least believe He was when I really didn't even believe that. Between sobs, I blurted out, "I do not believe. Help my unbelief!"

Saylor sat down beside me, put her arm around me, and whispered, "*Pistis*."

I looked at her, and she could see I was confused. All I could get out was, "What?"

"*Pistis*, Brea," Talya said. "*Divine evidence and conviction*. You would not be here if God had not spoken to you. The teaching and Scripture, 'All have sinned and fall short of the glory of God.' We, as our teachers have said, were in our past life. Godless without God. It was only when God came to us and stirred in our hearts planting His seeds that we began to come to life."

"It is the root understanding of *Pistis*, Brea," Saylor said as she pulled me a little closer. "If God had not spoken to your heart, you would not be on this quest. In fact, you would not have had one thought about Him. It is only as He speaks to you that you know to respond. If He did not initiate the conversation, you would never have had a conversation with Him. He is, after all, the beginning and the ending of all things. You doubt that He is, and yet the fact that you are here is proof that He is. Had He not spoken to your heart at some point, you would not have known to seek what you are currently seeking."

"It is so strange that most people of later times think it is all about them. They seem to think they are the god; it is as if their word is the authoritative word." Talya said, "It burdens them with weights they cannot carry. When the responsibility for our salvation rests on our shoulders, it is a burden that will crush us. The Pharisees learned that. Brother Nicodemus teaches that lesson. He is so funny to listen to; the man has such a great sense of humor, especially when he tells the story about his conversation with Jesus. You should have seen his facial expression when he said to Jesus, 'Surely, they cannot enter a second time into their mother's womb to be born!' (John 3:4b, NIV). He told us Jesus' expression was such that if the situation and teaching were not so important, he probably would have fallen on the ground laughing. Instead, Jesus was amazed at his inability to grasp the concept; after all, Nicodemus is a teacher of the law, and the purpose of the law was to expose our deadness in sin."

"I wouldn't be here if God had not spoken to me?" I said, puzzled over the idea that God had spoken to me.

"Brea," Saylor responded, "*Pistis*. Remember, it all begins with Divine. That is so important for you to remember; it all begins with Him. Have you ever felt the need to pray?"

"Of course I have!" I responded.

"And did you follow that feeling?" Saylor continued.

"Yes, well, at least most of the time," I said. Curiosity began to swell up inside of me. Where was she going with all of this?

The Word of God

"Based on what you have said so far, you probably started out trying to convince God to do the thing you felt you were supposed to pray about, didn't you?" Saylor questioned.

I paused to think back and said, "Yes, I did! Don't we all? I mean, after all, we need to let Him know what it is that we are asking for. How else are we supposed to get Him to do things? He can't do what He doesn't know we want Him to do."

Saylor smiled and said, "Brea, you are missing the point. Our teachers tell us to pray with faith, and believing. If you understood faith—to be Divine evidence and conviction—then you would understand that you wouldn't know to pray for a thing if God had not inspired you to pray for it in the first place. Once you understand that, your conversation with God becomes more of an inquiry as to how He wants to carry out the thing He inspired you to pray about. I have children, I know what they need before they ask, and I begin to do things that prompt them to ask. For example, I might begin to draw water because I know, from observing them, that they are thirsty. The same is true for food; I begin to prepare the meal before they ask because I know they are getting hungry. In your time, do parents not purchase items to feed their children before they are needed? For us to think God does not know our needs and begin to prepare the meal before we are even aware of our hunger shows our lack of understanding of our relationship with God. When we think we are the originators of our requests, it shows our belief that God does not know everything and does not know us."

Saylor continued, "Better than any good parent, God is watching over us and knows our needs before we ask, He prompts us to ask, or we wouldn't. Most people spend a lot of energy trying to convince God to do something they would not have thought to ask for if He hadn't placed in them that desire to ask. God is not a god who requires us to petition Him like the pagans petition their dead gods. God is alive and speaks to us all the time; sin prevents our hearing and understanding. Talya mentioned Nicodemus and his conversation about being born again. It is only when we have been brought to spiritual life that we begin to believe that God is and that He is the rewarder of those who diligently seek Him. Even that seeking is prompted by Him. Everything, and I mean everything that is good, comes from Him. Sin prevents us from seeing that. Sin is the darkness that blinds us. It is the work of the devil, and Jesus came to destroy that work."

"Diligently seek Him." I responded, "Isn't that what we are doing when we petition Him? I've heard people begging God for things. Are they wrong to do this? Isn't that diligently seeking Him?"

"Not really," Nolan replied, "to diligently seek Him would be to diligently seek what He wants. Most of the time, when people are begging God, they lack understanding. When you know that everything good and Holy comes directly from God, then you begin to realize that it is not a matter of us telling God what we want, but rather us diligently seeking His will in a situation, then asking Him to fulfill His desire, not ours. Many times, what we think is best is our idea of best, not His."

"If I understand what you are telling me, the very fact that I am here is proof that God spoke? This is not a quest that I initiated, but rather God started it?" I asked.

"Absolutely," Nolan responded. "All this time, you have been telling everyone you didn't believe that you couldn't believe. You have been asking God for proof or evidence that would allow you to believe. The truth of the matter is you know you don't believe because He has shown you your unbelief. All this time, your knowledge of your unbelief has been evidence that there is a God and that He has been speaking to you. Sadly, most fail to admit their unbelief, but they do, however, show it by *not* encouraging a person like you to ask God for evidence that will convince you of more."

"More what?" I asked.

"More evidence, Brea." Once again, Talya spoke up. "If people in your era understood and believed the words recorded in what is called the Bible, they should know that no one believes without evidence. We are incapable of believing without God enabling us or giving us evidence. Each time you realized you did not believe, God spoke to your heart, exposing what He knew all along was there—your unbelief. He has been speaking, or you wouldn't be seeing your unbelief."

Kolby couldn't keep quiet any longer and nearly shouted when he spoke, "You mean the reason the sword, which is the word, has no power is that we are using what was said to others instead of what is said to us?"

"Exactly," Saylor said, smiling like a teacher whose student finally got it.

"How does that make the word powerful and sharper?" Kolby asked.

"Kolby," Nolan chimed in, "Have you ever read a scripture verse, and something about it spoke to you directly at that moment? Maybe it was a verse you read before, possibly several times before; however, for some reason, at that moment, you heard its message as if for the first time?"

"Yes," Kolby replied.

"That is the living word, or the word brought to life by the presence and power of the Holy Spirit. That is why He is called the Spirit of life, or the Spirit that gives Life. Without the Spirit giving light, life, and power, none of us would know anything." Nolan said satisfied Kolby was finally catching on.

I rejoined the conversation. "From what you are saying,

I have been trying to get a God I did not believe in to give me evidence that would convince me that He really did exist when all along I wouldn't have recognized I didn't believe if He hadn't shown me that I didn't. It is like I was trying to get God to listen all this time when the real problem was that I wasn't listening? Or maybe the real problem was that those who were teaching me could not see what it was that not only me but probably most, if not all people, needed. We were not doubting, we were being honest; perhaps more honest than the teachers teaching us." I suddenly remembered Thomas and how everyone called him Doubting Thomas when in fact, he was Honest Thomas.

"Brea," Saylor said, "He is and always will be with you. Sin prevents us from seeing Him. Your teachers have been taught, and their teachers were taught. You see, truth is lost when tradition is followed without question. It is lost to the people until someone like you comes along and says, 'Enough, I will not be denied. I must see Jesus.' The Apostle Thomas teaches that. He was one of the first to do so because he, more than anyone, knew the importance of the evidence."

"Are you saying I'm the only one who is having trouble with this in my era?" I asked. I hoped this wasn't the case; if it was, then I was different and would continue to be alone.

"No, of course not, Brea," Talya comforted. "James

was always telling us, 'Faith without works is dead' (James 2:20, KJV). It is no less faith; it simply is dead. I would imagine there are a great number of people in your era struggling to believe. In fact, many of them have given up because there was no one there to tell them that they can have the evidence they need and require. The evidence all need, no matter how much evidence that is, is evidence that God wants and is willing to give them. Thomas required no less than the others; Jesus was willing and able to give it. Thomas was not required to blindly believe. You will share what you have and are about to learn when you return to Kayla, the Second Chance shop, and Chicago. There are those who want to believe but cannot, and they will seek you out. You will not have to seek them because they will find you."

"If there are more people than just me, why haven't I found them before?" I asked. It had me puzzled. How many people were struggling with belief like I was?

"Fear of people, Brea." Nolan stepped close to me and looked me in the eye as he spoke, "People don't want the group to know they are different. It takes courage to step up and say no to the crowd. Leaders dare to tread where others will not; it has always been that way and will always be. Many give up before they find."

He paused as if to pull from memory a story to help explain, then he continued, "There is an old story about a well near the far edge of the great desert. At the end of the desert was a land that promised great riches. The well was dug by the ancients. If a traveler did not drink from the well, they would not make it to the promised land. When the ancients dug it, the well water was deep down in the well, and a rope tied to a container was required to reach the water. As time went on, the rope broke and required someone to tie it. With the knot, the rope was shorter, and eventually, after enough knots were tied, the water could no longer be reached with the rope, and an outstretched arm was needed to draw water from the well. Each desert traveler would stop by the well and draw its life-giving water; however, as years passed, the water became more difficult to reach due to the knots added by new generations. After many years those who lacked desire began to die of thirst because they failed to lengthen the rope; the water was still in the same place. They thought, *Surely the rope is long enough; the well must be dry.* With that idea, they would lie down and eventually die, but not before they had passed on the story of the dry well. When the next traveler came by the well, saw the dead bodies, and heard the story that by now was the traditional story, they determined the well must be dry. They, too, would lie down and eventually die. After a great many had fallen by the well, one traveler crossed the desert, came to the well, and lowered the bucket but found no water. It happened that one of the previous travelers was still clinging to life. He shared with the new arrival the traditional story of a dry well passed down from one traveler to the next seeking water; they passed down the tradition of a dry well, not of life-giving water."

I was saddened by the story, knowing it was mine. Nolan continued, "This new arrival listened as the sad tale was told, and he was distraught, knowing his fate lay at the top of the well with the multitude of dead. Then a thought came to him, if he died there by the well, wild animals would tear his flesh, and maybe they would do it before he expired. His thirst grew as he stood listening to the traditional story. As he thought, he asked, 'What has been done that determined the well is empty?' The mentor told him how two before him let down the rope halfway and drew no water. The one after him let it down three-quarters, and finally, the mentor himself let the rope down all the way with an outstretched arm, only to find no water, evidence the well was dry. The new arrival walked over to the well, untied the rope from its secure anchor, let the bucket down to the end of the rope and his outstretched arm, turned and looked at his dying mentor, smiled, and said, 'I will not be denied.' With that, he jumped into the well, following the rope and bucket to the bottom. In horror, the mentor mourned the tragic loss of this newcomer. With his last breath, the mentor heard a splash as the newcomer found water where others could not because they lacked the courage to leap."

Nolan tilted his head slightly, looked deeper into my eyes as if to see my heart, and said, "You see, Brea, it takes courage, a hunger, and a thirst to leap where others fear to go when tradition tells you the well is empty. It really comes down to whether you are willing to throw yourself down the proverbial well to get what you are thirsting for."

At that moment, all the years of seeking what I could not find began to weigh even heavier on me. It felt as if I were suffocating, as if an elephant had settled on my chest, and my lungs could not find enough oxygen to sustain life. Deep in my being, I realized I was thirsty. I felt as if I had crossed Nolan's desert and was standing at the edge of the well. At that same time, a hunger far worse than anything I had ever felt made itself known. This was a deeper pain than I had ever experienced in my life. *What was it I needed? What could possibly be out there that would satisfy this thing that appeared to be my deepest desire?* I thought as I considered Nolan's question.

Suddenly the thought came to me, and I said, "But Nolan, Jesus said, 'Because you have seen me, you have believed. Blessed are those who have not seen, and have believed.' (John 20:29 WEB) That says we should believe without seeing."

"Thomas saw the physical Jesus, but that does not mean we are not to expect spiritual evidence. You see, Brea, Jesus was pointing to the next level of evidence that God would give. Not that physical evidence is excluded, but rather deeper personal evidence that would not leave with the accumulation of events. Physical appearances and acts such as miracles are forgotten and challenged after a few generations. However, when each generation receives the miraculous evidence, the promise of the Father, the Holy Spirit, it is proof that Jesus is the Messiah and alive ever making intercession for us. When our first parents fell and were driven from the garden, the Holy Spirit was withdrawn from them. As a result, they lost their holiness. Jesus instructed the disciples to wait in Jerusalem for the promise of the Father, the Holy Spirit. He, the Holy Spirit, is the evidence that cannot be seen with the eye."

Up to that point, I had been thrust into the battlefields. They caused me great anxiety and fear. Suddenly I realized something, something very terrifying; those battles were showing me what I lacked, the shield that could not protect, and even after I discovered the meaning of the name on the shield, it still lacked power. Kolby's sword wasn't as sharp as it was before; why? Did we have to return to the battle willingly? Was it amid the battle that we would find our answer? I turned loose of the shield. I had to talk to Kayla. I needed advice and support. Instantly, I was standing in the Second Chance shop. Kayla was smiling and holding out the bag bearing my name. "I feel as if I must enter the battle willingly to get what I need, should I?" These were the first words out of my mouth.

"My dear," Kayla said, "this bag contains items you have placed in it over the years. With each new item placed in the bag, it grew heavier. Take it, and see for yourself; it weighs more now than when you first entered the shop. You refused it then; will you be willing to take it now?"

"I asked you a question, and you offer me that bag? What kind of answer is that?" I reluctantly asked. I did not understand. Why couldn't she just tell me? Why did everything have to be complicated?

"Things of great value are always hidden from the casual onlooker, Brea. This bag is your battle; you have refused and resisted it up till now. My answer to you is here; by offering it, I have answered your question."

Without hesitation, I reached out, took hold of the bag, grabbed the shield, and instantly was standing on the battlefield. I opened the drawstring on the bag, looked deeply into it, and things began to float up out of it. Every disappointment I had ever experienced, every hurt that I had harbored in my heart, suddenly floated up in front of me. As I examined it, pain shot up from my inner core, and I felt the first arrow strike me. I glanced down and saw a word written on it. I read it out loud "Unworthy." Then I realized that where the arrow had lodged was the same place it had struck in a previous battle. Then another fiery dart struck me and sank even deeper. I looked, and it, too, had a word on it. I read it out loud, "Unloved."

Suddenly, the arrows started coming so fast that it seemed like they were being fired from a machine gun. I raised the shield, hoping it would protect me, but it did not. I realized it was useless; it lacked the ability to protect me. I became aware of Kayla standing next to me, not protecting me but pouring something over me. It was cool; it ran down from my head to my feet. It was red; it was the blood that I had seen in the previous battle; however, now it was not protecting. Arrows were passing right through it, striking my heart. I looked up at Kayla; she was looking up as if gazing into heaven itself. She was saying something, but I could not make out the words she was speaking. Another arrow or dart or whatever struck me again. I thought, *Why isn't she protecting me from this like she did before?*

I was beginning to weaken; darkness was closing in around me. Not just darkness but saddening, sickening darkness that was oppressive. I sensed I was speaking, but without words, it was a guttural moan more than speaking. I could not articulate what I was feeling; it was a request, that I was sure of, but what was it I was asking? Then I saw it, a path; what in the world was going on? This was probably the weirdest thing that had happened so far. Something told me I had been asking for something; apparently, what I had asked for was a way because it was clear that I was supposed to take this path.

You might think I'm crazy, but I could have sworn there was a sign lighted and flashing like the open sign in the window of the Second Chance shop. This sign, however, said, "Walk it." Now, mind you, while all of this was going on, the battle, the arrows, the blood, all of that was still happening; yet somehow, I discovered I had the ability to stand up and walk. The battlefield was still very much happening, yet I was walking down the path. It was unbelievable, but I knew it was happening. I brushed my hands against a thorny bush on the side of the path; I looked over the bush, and to my amazement, there were acres of thorny bushes choking out all other life. Seeds were falling into the thorns, but with the thickness of the thorns, nothing was taking root, and no light could get in.

As I walked, I passed a huge area filled with stones, rocks, and boulders. There in that field, I could see small startup vegetation. It was odd, to say the least. However, I was sure it was happening; seeds were falling from somewhere and sprouting up immediately. As soon as they sprouted, the hot sun would cause them to wither, and they would die.

I continued my walk and passed by an area that had not been cultivated. Seeds were falling on it as well. They did not sprout; the birds were plucking the seeds up and eating them. I finally saw a man who appeared to be the source of the seeds. He was spreading them everywhere and walking nearly parallel to me.

I looked out ahead of him and saw a field that appeared to have been freshly plowed. Whoever the farmer was, he or she had taken great care to prepare the soil and make it ready for planting. The man sowing the seeds was walking right toward it. I knew he would finally be able to plant the seeds in some fertile, well-prepared soil. Something down deep inside me started to get excited, and I started to walk faster toward the field that was ready to take in the seeds and produce a crop. I ran into the field, sat down, and lifted my head and hands up as if to receive the seeds from the hand of the Sower.

As the Sower passed by me, I looked up and was blinded by the light shining around him. I couldn't see his face, but something told me he was kind and gentle, taking careful aim to ensure the seeds would fall into my hands. No, not my hands, deeper; he was aiming at my lips, and I sensed the seed needed to enter me. Then I heard it. His voice said my name, "Brea." That was all he said, and as soon as he did, one of the seeds passed over my lips and lodged down in my chest. The moment it lodged in my heart, a joy I had never experienced sprang up like a plant breaking the surface of the ground. At that moment, I felt love, love like a river flowing out of that seed in my chest.

I know you will probably doubt what I am telling you, but at that moment, everything changed. I saw things for the first time, things I was not aware of before. I was like a baby coming from the womb, being born, and seeing the world for the first time. I felt peace, like a gentle breeze blowing over me, and that love, that incredible love that would not stop. It was gushing out like a geyser, and the pressure down inside was enormous; I even tried to stop it and could not. At that point, I said to myself, "Let it go, Brea. Don't resist it; enjoy it. Brea Rea Joyce, your name is written in a book that will last forever."

Then, I heard it; a voice, like that of an angel, no, it was more powerful and clear, there was no mistaking it, the voice said, "Brea, let me introduce you to your Father. You are His child; know that you are loved! At that moment, I cried 'Abba Father,' and the voice of His Spirit testified with my spirit that I was indeed a child of God."

With that, everything went into hyperdrive. Suddenly I was back on the battlefield, lying on the ground, arrows sticking out all over me. The enemy was standing over me, smiling a wicked smile, his sword drawn, and in a swift movement, he swung it at my chest. That enemy was so evil and large. Just as the blade was ready to strike my chest, quicker than light speed, my left hand raised the shield, and the enemy's sword struck the shield with an impact that sounded like thunder. The shield glowed with white light like lightning, and flashes of light exploded as the enemy's sword struck it. I barely felt the impact; in fact, I started to laugh, and I heard myself saying, "Enough."

At that moment, the enemy stepped back and drew back his bow loaded with the deadliest arrow I had ever seen. He released it, and the arrow shot right toward my heart. As if by instinct, my right hand grabbed a sword sheathed at my back. I thought to myself, *Where did that sword come from?* My hand pulled the sword from the sheath in a fluid motion; I swung it and split the arrow from the head through the fletching. The arrow split into two parts, one shooting off to the left and the other to the right; they bounced off metal plates that were covering my upper arm. This time the split arrow did not leave a mark; it simply flew off in two different directions.

I looked at the sword in my hand, and it was glowing-white hot, sharper than anything I had ever seen. Both sides were sharp, a double-edged sword. I laughed and knew that the enemy was defeated. He fled, dissolved like a vapor.

I turned to my left, and standing next to me was Kayla, young Kayla, battle-ready Kayla, fierce fighting Kayla. Interestingly, I saw her sword reach out and split an arrow that was just about to pierce an old man lying on the ground. The arrow split, and each half struck the arm of the man; he cringed as the arrow burnt through the flesh on his arm, leaving a mark as it had me just a short time ago.

To my right, I saw Kolby. In his hand was a double-edged sword, sharper than anything I had seen before. Well, at least that I hadn't seen until my own appeared. He swung it and split an arrow whose direction went just like the one Kayla had split, except Kolby was protecting a young woman who was lying on the ground.

CHAPTER 10
CHOICE

Instantly, a flash of light rippled across the battlefield, and the scene changed. All three of us were sitting in a field filled with flowers and soft grasses. Kolby was sitting on a small boulder, Kayla was reclining against another, and I was perched on a small branch protruding from a tree growing next to the stream that slowly rippled by us.

Kolby spoke first. "Amazing," he said. "The word of God, living, speaking not once but continuously, that is what I was missing. Up to this point in my life, all I knew was what was written. Today I have the word spoken to me. I heard it, believed it, and now I have it. It is mine, and it gave power to the sword, which is the word of God. This is what was missing from my life. My quest is now complete. I am satisfied. I will live my life knowing what gives the word power. It is not just what was said; it must be empowered by what is said by God to the hearts of people. If the word of God does not speak to my heart, then the words I read are simply words. Only when the living God empowers the recorded words or the words spoken to my heart do they have the ability to slice through even the toughest of material to illuminate and give wisdom. Brea, I am so glad you brought me along on this journey, and look, I, too, have a shield of my very own. See the nameplate PISTIS, but check this out; down at the very bottom, it says 'Brea.' I think it is a reminder that it all started with your shield; when I didn't have a shield, you gave me a part of yours. Thank you, I will never forget you."

"Kolby, that is so sweet of you. It has been a joy to travel with you, and I rejoice in your victory," I replied.

"Kayla," I said, "Thank you so much for your wisdom and kindness to me. I need to ask you one more thing. The bag you gave me, when I took it, the thing was so heavy I could hardly keep it off the ground. Now it is nearly empty; why is that?"

Kayla smiled and said, "Brea, that bag is your heart. It was burdened down with all the things that have ever hurt you. Each time something happened, you put it away in your heart; it began to weigh you down. It found lodging in a place that keeps a record of every wrong that has ever come against you. Now, however, you are new, a new person; born again, born from above, born not by human decision, but born of God by the Spirit of God. The old passed away, and all things have become new. The life you now live, you live by the power of the Blood. Enjoy!"

"This is incredible," I said. "I never knew that such a life existed. All the people I have encountered over the years seemed to be lacking something. I think what they were missing was the joy and peace that I now am enjoying."

"You might be surprised by how many you have met who actually had and or have what you now have, Brea." Kayla said, "Your eyes are now opened, and you will see what you could not see before. Many of the people you meet have what you have but do not know what it is that they have. They try to share it with others but simply cannot find the words and have not had the teaching that can assist them. I met a woman who found exactly what you have; I took her through the Scriptures and pointed out the words of Jesus, the Apostle Paul, Peter, James, and John. Words that are recorded in the Bible, words that were written to assist people and lead them to a place where those words are brought to life by the power of the Holy Spirit. Once taught, she was able to find not only satisfaction in what she had, but she also discovered power, for knowing that her spiritual experience was the born-again experience, she had the power to resist the enemy when he attempted to disrupt her joy."

"It's sad," I replied, "that the teaching of my current time has lost this valuable truth, it has become nothing more than human teaching and human decision."

Kolby laughed and said, "Brea, it is not something that happened in your time; consider my quest. The truth was lost to me as well. Perhaps the world goes through these times. The truth is revealed to one generation that is hungry and seeking; they have the experience. The next generation develops a doctrine, and the next has only the doctrine, then, at some point, two or three generations later, a person or a people arise hungry for the truth, and history repeats itself."

Kayla added, "There is always a remnant preserved. Sadly, their message is buried like a treasure waiting for someone to discover it. When they do, they are either the next generation or the remnant."

"So, what am I?" I was eager to know if this was going to be a solo flight or if I would have many who would join me.

"That, my dear, is something that is hidden in the future. Perhaps you will one day learn to travel there and bring back the knowledge of what is to come. For now, rejoice in the fact that your name is written in the Lambs Book of Life. Who or how many will come along with you on this journey may rest in your hands as well as God's. If you look at what Jesus said in His generation, you must believe it is true of all generations."

"And what is it that you are referring to, Kayla?" Her words were still a bit mysterious to me, but I was learning at a very fast pace.

"Surely you remember His words to the disciples:

'they are ripe for harvest' (John 4:35, NI). It is repeated in Revelations 14:15. There has always been a great hunger in the world; sadly, there are those who exploit that and turn many away from the truth. Consider this, in the world's past, things moved slower than they do in your time, Brea. Kolby, for example, travels by horse or on foot. The message moves at a slower speed than in your age. You can travel near light speed." Kayla continued to add more mystery even in her answering my question.

Kolby's eyes opened wide with amazement, and he blurted out, "What do you mean light speed? What is light speed?"

Kayla and I both laughed. Neither of us realized that Kolby would have no knowledge of light speed in his time. Kayla did her best to explain, "Kolby, if you are on a hill at night, there is a valley between you and another hill, and someone lights a candle on the other hill, how long does it take you to see it from the time they light the candle?"

"I've never thought of such a thing, Kayla. Light is instant." Kolby said, bewildered by the mere thought of such a thing.

"That doesn't surprise me," I replied, "The fact that light travels at a certain speed is not discovered until four hundred years after your time."

Kolby looked a little saddened by the thought that he would miss out on the things of the future and said, "Why was I born too soon?"

Kayla responded, "You have just discovered that there is a God, which means there is also an eternity, Kolby. Time does not exist where death does not exist. When you pass from this life into the next, all these things will be revealed to you. Brea has simply plucked you from your time to allow you to discover what it was you were seeking. She found you because you were looking for her. If you hadn't followed my advice, you would not have stepped outside the camp and met her. You will return to your time with the knowledge that others do not have. Be very careful who you share these things with and how you share them. Those of your time will not understand. They will think you a wizard and seek to end your life as well as your message."

With that, Kayla turned back to me and said, "Brea, your phone allows you to travel near light speed. The internet provides you with a pathway into the homes and lives of people around the world. You enter it on your computer, press save or send, and almost instantly, they see it. Because of the speed with which you may travel, your era is ripe for a bountiful harvest. While I cannot tell you what will be, I can tell you what is available to you and encourage you to use it to your advantage. Books are another great way to share your story. Dub it fiction, fill it with facts, and people will discover what they will. The message that falls on hard ground will be plucked up by the birds; the message that falls on rocky soil will sprout quickly but wither. Some will fall on thorny ground and be choked out. Each of these soils is in the heart of individuals at different stages of their life. At one point, you were in each of these conditions; as of late, God prepared the soil of your heart to receive the seed. The more you share what you have discovered, the more you will harvest."

"Me? Write a book?" I queried, "I was hoping at some point in my life to be able to write a great paper that would allow people to view some truth I discovered in an ancient artifact; however, I was not thinking of a book."

"Didn't you discover an ancient artifact? You did, through your search. Did you not discover a truth that people of your era do not seem to know? A truth that has been lost?" Kayla asked.

"You're right, Kayla," I exclaimed. "I forgot that is exactly what just took place. A book, hmm… That is appealing, a fiction book that is fact-filled. I like that type of book; it always makes me wonder if it is fiction or fact."

"Perhaps it is both." Kayla mused, "I believe a lot of fiction in your grandparent's day has become a reality in yours, so why not this?"

"That settles it, Kayla. I'm going to write a book about this quest I have been on. I'll make up names and inject actual stories and conversations I've had with those I have met along the way." I replied. I was getting excited about the idea, even as I was telling Kayla about it. Something inside of me anchored down in my spirit, and I knew I would one day write the book.

"Don't forget me when you write your book, Brea." Kolby said, then added, "Make sure you let your readers know I was the 'Ninja Knights Templar.' I so like the sound of that." He chuckled and repeated the word Ninja over and over.

"Remember what I said, Kolby; use caution when talking about your journey. People in your day are not as open to time travel as they are in Brea's." Kayla warned, somehow, she knew he was going to secretly call himself 'The Ninja Knights Templar' even if no one else knew.

"Kolby, as much as I would like us to linger here, I think it is time you got about your business. Remember what you have learned; decide how you can best share it in your time. Use caution when you return. There are those who seek to destroy those who are bearers of the truth, and those destroyers come in many different forms." Kayla's words to Kolby were solemn and a bit sad.

I got up from my little perch and walked over to Kolby. He stood, put his arms around me, and gave me a hug. The scene resembled a big brother heading off to war, saying farewell to his little sister. I felt such a connection to him. We had been through so much together. How far he had come from his Templar rules and regulations about women. We were united in a way that I felt would transcend time.

Kolby kissed me on the cheek and said, "Farewell, little

sister, till we meet again." With that, he turned loose of his shield and was gone.

Tears began to flow down my cheeks; I was emotionally aching as if I were separated from my big brother. I missed him already. I turned to Kayla and said, "I suppose we are ready to go as well."

I turned loose of the shield and once again was in the Second Chance shop. This time, however, Kayla was still in her young self-body, full battle gear, a flaming sword, and a shining shield. "I'm so proud of you, Brea. You have done well, and you have crossed over from unbelief to belief. Realize that what you are now in possession of, everyone needs. None can believe without the living word of God spoken directly from Him to their hearts. Those who will not seek this are not ready. Those who have it and do not know it will need your guidance, and those who seek it need your leadership so they may find it," Kayla said.

"Before I stepped into your shop Kayla, I had no idea what was wrong with me. Now that I have taken this journey, I realize that the faith taught today has only two elements; the first is our belief, and the second is our trust. Those two things are not enough; we need the *third element*, which is the first element. People have been placed under a great heavy burden when religious teachers have failed to understand their own words or at least the words they read."

"The third element," Kayla inquired.

"Yes," I replied, "*Divine evidence and conviction* is the thing that produces belief and trust. My era defined faith with only two elements, our belief, and our trust. Without the third element, which is the first, whatever it is we have, it is not the biblical understanding of faith. In fact, as I think about it, if we do not give credit to God for what we have, we are, in a sense, stealing from Him." My response was more a question than a statement.

"I see," Kayla said thoughtfully, "and you think this third element will make a difference?"

"Of course, it will. In my day, we have all but eliminated the involvement of God in the salvation process, or at least relegated it to the recorded past. Most say they believe; however, if God does not reveal Himself to us, we may as well believe in fairies. The Divine evidence and conviction God gives us enable belief and trust. Those who think they believe because they have made the decision to, or those who follow Christ because they decided to, are no better than a servant. I realize now without the Spirit of Adoption declaring me God's child, I am not; the Apostle Paul tells us that in Romans 8. All of what I have is dependent on what He says about the matter. None of this has to do with what I decide; no more than a child can say to a stranger, 'I chose you as my father or mother.' The parent is the one who has the power to adopt." I was beginning to develop a sense of flow that would enable me to give an answer for the faith I had.

Kayla tilted her head and looked me over; you could tell she was determining her next words. "But, Brea, we do have a choice in the matter; otherwise, we are nothing more than puppets. If our choice is not a part of this process, then we are not free."

"Hmm," I responded, thinking about what she was saying. "Perhaps our decision is only to follow, and even that is because He enables us to stand up and walk. If we are truly dead in our sins, what part does the dead person play in reviving?"

"You must remember we are only dead in the spiritual sense, not the physical or conscious, and so long as we are living in this physical body, we make choices. Those choices would have to include moral ones. While we might be born under the curse of Adam, we are not, by that, condemned as guilty in God's sight. The choice to follow that nature handed down from our forefathers is pollution and not a thing that would condemn. Condemnation must come to us as the result of actions deriving from our choices. Therefore, choice must be a part of our message to the world." Kayla's words sank deep into my mind, and I believe they settled into that place where conviction is recorded.

"I see what you mean, Kayla," I said, considering her words. "I can't seem to wrap my head around how choice mingles with faith. None of this would have been necessary if this simply boiled down to my choice. That was the entire problem I was dealing with. I could not make that choice without assistance from God, and nothing I did resulted in belief. Where is the choice in that?"

"If you think about it," Kayla replied, "you did make a choice. You simply were not aware of how you were choosing to follow. You see, God intended to make you His child, not His servant. A servant is either forced or makes a choice, while a child is born into the family. The word justification means…"

At that point, I interrupted and quoted something I had been taught when I was a child "I know justification means, 'Just as if I never sinned.' I remember that from my childhood teaching."

"Tradition versus truth, Brea!" Kayla responded, a little put out with me falling back into a traditional teaching that could not bring satisfaction to my heart. "The word justification means to pardon and accept. The scripture is quite clear on who pardons and accepts; it is God who justifies. It is not the result of human decisions or the will of a parent. In other words, we are not born into it because we made a choice or because our parents follow it."

"Wait a minute, Kayla," I was now starting to challenge her. "You just told me choice does play a part, and now you are saying it does not. I am confused." I did not mean to sound harsh, but this was starting to sound a lot like the stuff I was running from.

"You must keep in mind all of what the Scripture says about faith. Faith can either be living or dead. It is no less faith; it is simply living or dead. A person might have the Divine evidence and conviction and choose to do nothing with it; as a result, they still have faith; it is just dead."

Kayla paused for a moment to allow me to process this, then continued, "The person who receives a revelation provided by God and chooses to act on what has been revealed; they have living faith. To which God will typically respond with more revelation. It is a life lived, Brea; God reveals, we see, we respond, and He gives more. A life of faith is a life of living in revelation from God and taking steps in keeping with that revelation. Two things can come into play; first, you do not have enough revelation, and second, you are not mature enough to handle it. You will find inside of you there is still a thing that sides with your enemy. Up to this point, you struggled to believe God is and to believe you were God's child. How is it that you know it now?"

"I know it because He told me so. In addition to that, He gave me His Spirit as a deposit guaranteeing my inheritance," I replied.

"In the past, you were challenged by the enemy as to whose child you were. In fact, you did not believe that God existed until He (God) broke the silence and poured forth an utterance. Your believer was not broken; it is and was perfectly fine. You, however, like Thomas, were lacking proof, not physical proof but spiritual proof. You were like a fetus in the womb, connected but not yet born. In the past, each time the enemy challenged you, you were defeated because, at that time, all you could use to defend yourself was hope, and that was not strong enough to win the battle. As a result, you would collapse back into unbelief. The cycle continued and increased your frustration; Without any proof or evidence, you had nothing to defend yourself. We both know that did not work for you."

Kayla was spot on and continued, "Now, however, you have Divine Evidence and a deep conviction, which was placed there by the presence of the Holy Spirit within. When that evidence came to you, you could have refused to believe it, or you could have claimed the revelation was of your own doing as the result of your own efforts; either way, you would have been in the same position as before. Somewhere along your journey, God gave you enough evidence to persuade you He was indeed real and that you were, in fact, His child. At that moment, belief and trust sprang to life because of the Divine evidence you received, and it drove deep into your being where convictions are created. All these things have to do with Faith, both the Divine evidence and conviction, as well as the choice to believe. Remember Thomas and your conversation with him?"

"Of course I do. It made me see him in a different light; instead of Doubting Thomas, I now see him as Honest Thomas." As I responded, my mind wandered back to my meeting with Thomas, and I recalled him stating he needed the same thing the other Apostles needed, to see Jesus.

Kayla continued, "Then, you recall his words regarding all of us needing proof to ensure what was said was real. Having gained that evidence, he believed; we know this because Jesus declared it. Jesus also said, 'Blessed are those who have not seen and yet believe' (John 20:29, NIV). They are the ones, like yourself, who realized that without some proof, they could not believe, that is to say, if God be real, let Him show Himself to me, help my unbelief. If you look through the Bible, at no point did God change things and require us to start the conversation with Him, nor did or does He ask us to trust without providing some type of evidence that would enable that trust. This is true not only of those born after Jesus' time on earth but from the beginning. Adam and Eve, in whatever form they resided, failed to retain the knowledge of God. Sadly, that failure brought about a great many sorrows. One of the things it did was render us Godless or without God. The only way to remedy that was through ongoing contact and communication with Him. Whether you choose to continue to believe the evidence, despite what may seem like contradictions or proof against it, it is inevitably your choice. Does that make sense to you?"

I sometimes joke that my slowness to catch on is the

result of my blondness; the truth is I process things and run through a series of mental experiments, which takes some time to complete, which slows my understanding and responses to things. Sadly, when I am not slow to respond, it usually gets me into trouble. As Kayla was speaking, the wheels were churning, and ultimately the mental experiments ended just as she asked the question, and I was able to happily respond, "Yes, that does make sense."

"It is extremely important for you to see the flow of this." Kayla was very serious as she spoke, "Remember, it all starts with the Divine or God, He provides the evidence, and that generates a conviction. We, in response, are enabled to make decisions or choices based on the evidence received and recognized."

"Yes, I understand, and the flow makes sense now." I truly was understanding and was happy she took the time to explain.

"One more thing, Brea." With those words, I sat up on the edge of my chair, sensing our conversation was about to end. Kayla continued, "Not everyone needs the same amount of evidence; each of us is different. While you require what some might consider dramatic proof, others need very little; their childlike innocence allows them to believe without a great amount of proof. Do not fall under the trap some have succumbed to. There are a great many who limit the revelations of God to certain evidence, such as particular gifts, words, or revelations afforded at the time a person is enabled to move from unbelief to belief. One person's evidence is rarely the same as another's. There is, however, a common thread that unifies us. That common thread is the Love of God poured into our hearts by the Holy Spirit, the Spirit of Adoption. The process is always the same so that no one can boast. God sheds His love abroad in your heart, revealing your new status as a child of God; in that same instance, your spirit testifies with God's Spirit that you are a child of God. The presence of the Holy Spirit always produces the fruit of the Spirit. You will see the difference as you continue this journey. The living can always recognize the dead; it is the dead who cannot see. Be careful to always follow the Spirit."

At that, we stood to our feet, Kayla and I hugged, and she said, "We will meet again!"

CHAPTER 11

FOLLOW WHERE IT LEADS

With that, she was gone. I stood there in the store alone, yet not alone; I knew I was not alone and would never be alone again. Suddenly, the scene changed. I shook my head as if to clear my senses. I looked down at my phone and could not believe what I was seeing; I had entered the store at 10 a.m. on Saturday morning, and my phone now read 10:07 a.m. that same Saturday morning. How could this have been possible? As I looked around the area where the shop was, I realized it was an alley between two buildings; I was at the backside of the alley. I placed both my hands on the side of my head and slowly let them slide down my face to my chin, holding them there; I was stunned. All that had taken place, it all transpired in seven minutes. Was none of it real?

At that moment, something miraculous happened.

Down deep in my heart, soul, or whatever you want to call it, something was different. The ache of my heart, the heaviness I used to feel, the doubt that always lingered there was gone. Instead, I felt this incredible love, and a still, small voice continued to declare me a child of the Living God. I knew, for the first time in my life, God was real, and I was His. Whatever else had just happened, that one thing was real above all else. I walked out of the alley, and the warm morning sun peeked out from behind one of the tall buildings. As the sun crossed my path, something caught my eye, like the shimmer from a shiny metal object. I looked down and discovered two metal protective bracelets on my forearm. They were the bracelets worn by a Roman Soldier. Normally, I would have been horrified, but for some reason, at that moment, I had assurance that something miraculous had just taken place.

My stomach gave me the notification that it needed to be filled. I looked around, and on the corner of Michigan and State streets was a small café. I walked the short few blocks and entered the café, placed my order, walked to a vacant table, and waited for my order to be delivered.

At the table next to me was a young woman in her early twenties. We smiled and greeted each other in the normal way. Sitting at the table with her was a woman in her early forties; she appeared to be the younger woman's mother. She stared at me as if I had two heads or something. She leaned over to her daughter and whispered something, to which the daughter shook her head, indicating no. I looked at them and said, "Is everything alright?"

The younger woman said, "Sorry, my name is Cindy, and this is my mother, Bonnie. Mom seems to be having an issue with how you are dressed."

I responded, "My name is Brea. What is the issue?"

Cindy shifted slightly in her chair. I could tell she was uncomfortable and hesitant to tell me what her mother was saying. Bonnie, on the other hand, was not as bashful and said, "Why are you dressed like a Roman Soldier?"

At that, Cindy buried her face in her hands, trying to hide the embarrassment she felt due to her mother asking such a silly question. Cindy said, "Mother, what is wrong with you? Brea is dressed in normal clothes; in fact, I think it is quite cute. I love the leather vest, and those boots are awesome; where did you find them?"

Bonnie blurted out, "No, she isn't dressed in a vest and boots; she is wearing a Roman Soldier outfit complete with shield and sword."

I was mystified; I looked down at my clothing and saw only the outfit I had dressed in before I left my condo, nothing Roman about it. Realizing something was happening that I had not experienced before, I decided it was better to carry on the conversation from one table instead of two; I felt Bonnie might have a story to tell. I said, "Would it be okay if I joined you at your table?"

Both women nodded yes, so I stood and moved to their table and sat next to Bonnie. I put my hand over her hand and said, "Bonnie, are you struggling with something?"

At that, Bonnie began to tell me how her marriage of twenty-five years had ended a few weeks ago when her husband unexpectedly died. She was trying to cope, but her anchor in life, her partner and best friend, was gone. Tears began to flow down her cheeks, and she said, "I want to believe things will be okay, but something down deep inside of me seems broken. I just can't believe!"

Our conversation was interrupted by the waitress delivering my breakfast. It seemed to break whatever was happening here at the table; Bonnie was drying her eyes when Cindy sat back in her chair with her mouth and eyes wide open and said, "Mother, you are right. Brea is dressed as a Roman Soldier!"

I sensed there was more to Bonnie's story than had been revealed. I asked the waitress for a to-go box, and she scurried off to fill my request. I said to the two women, "I don't live far from here. Would you like to come over to my condo, and we can talk in a more private location?"

Both agreed, and after a short walk, we were in my condo.

A Word from the Author

Brea's journey is not over; it is just beginning. If you enjoyed *Pistis the Third Element,* and or if this book has helped you in your personal journey, please let me know. You may email me at **soltow53@gmail.com** or learn more at **www.terrancesoltow.com**.

Please leave a review. It may encourage others to read this series.

You can catch a glimpse of Brea in the book *The Migdal Journals, Volume 1: The Journey Begins*, and Volume 2 of *The Migdal Journals* will be available soon.

Will there be a second Pistis book? Yes, the story is not over! You can continue to journey with Brea, many of her old friends, and some new ones in *Pistis the Third Element, Volume 2: Discovery.*

SOME THOUGHTS:
WHAT IS REAL AND WHAT IS FICTION

The characters: names and characters are, for the most part, fictional.

The storyline: The story contains truths. These truths are woven into a fictional story with the hope that it was fun reading but also that it would open the reader's heart and mind, allowing them to journey outside the camp and dwell in the tent of God.

The individual stories: The individual stories and testimonies found in chapter one are real and were put together from the real-life struggles of people I have dealt with over forty-plus years of ministry. My own story can be found among them.

Theological conversations: Many of the theological conversations between characters in this book were conversations I have had with others. Some are the result of my study and search for true faith. Other conversations and arguments were ones I have had with Abba, Father God. If you challenge the theology in this book, I encourage you to ask the question Brea asks, which is the same question I have had to ask many times. "Am I challenging this because it is false? Or am

I challenging it because it does not align with traditional teaching?"

Time-traveling characters: If the Bible is to be believed, Jesus was met by Moses and Elijah, and their appearance was witnessed by Peter, James, and John. Jesus appeared to the Apostle Paul on the road to Damascus; history has been peppered with people who claim to have met and conversed with the ancients. The book of Hebrews declares we are surrounded by a great cloud of witnesses. Most would tell you this is figurative; however, traditional teaching is what they use to support this, the words of the Bible, from which the traditional Christian teaching in some form is based, contradicts tradition in the above-stated instances. Science has discovered a field many call the Zero Point Field; you can read about it if you are interested. If science is correct, and you and I could tap into the ZPF, we could quite likely travel, if not in body, at least in some form, to the past and future. In ancient times they believed in a force field they called the Ether, which may very well be the ZPF.

Time: There are several theories about time, and as science continues to probe an area called the quantum realm, they have come to understand time has no significance and disappears at the quantum level. What many fail to understand is that what we perceive as reality is built out of the material of the quantum realm. If you think about time, it really is nothing more than a placeholder created by humans attempting to corral a concept that is beyond our understanding.

Pistis: is the Greek word that we translate as "faith." *Pistis* really does find its roots in evidence and conviction. The lost third element is real. The Hebrew word we translate faith is *emunah* which means "faithful." However, it, too, has been diluted by our current definition of faith. *Emunah* was a call to be faithful, remembering what God has done in the past. You cannot remember what you have not known. To know that God has done something in the past, you must have experienced it. The entire matter rests on God breaking the silence and pouring forth an utterance. The Psalmist calls us to "Taste and see that the LORD is Good" (Psalms 34:8, NIV). When you begin to recognize God as the author of these things, life really can change.

Lost third element: Is it lost? Perhaps. Maybe it is more the result of traditional teaching that some of us have been burdened with. History is filled with generations that have lost a true understanding of faith. Failing to understand that every thought we have about God is initiated by Him places the responsibility of belief back on us. In truth, we wouldn't believe if He had not provided enough information to enable us to believe. If we stop taking credit for what we did not do, we find a world of discovery open to us like never before. When we understand that we believe as a response to evidence and conviction He has given us, it provides unshakable confidence; if it is not enough evidence, we can simply ask for more; at some point, He will break the silence and pour forth the utterance.

Accepting Jesus as your personal Savior: I've always been curious about this. I kept looking at history and found an interesting turning point. I believe this current practice found its footing in the US in the latter part of the 18th century. A former lawyer turned preacher called upon his hearers to make their "decision." After his first message, the town's people nearly ran him out of the community because it appeared to be a new message. However, he had a second meeting at the conclusion of which he made the same demand, and some prominent people, not having Pistis, felt compelled and did as commanded. The rest is history. The man's name was Charles Finney. You can read it for yourself. I'm not sure Finney meant for this appeal to "make a decision" to be the end all, but rather the beginning of the journey that would ultimately culminate in the outpouring of the Holy Spirit, thus producing salvation. It appeared to me that after time his true call to decide became an end, not a beginning. Finney himself decided not to stop seeking God until God broke the silence and gave him some evidence. Finney's story is worth reading. Like a lot of other things, his message was most likely picked up by others who did not understand or sought to cash in on something that was working, and a tradition was born. This was not the first time something like this had happened. The Apostle Paul found many who sought the power of the Holy Spirit for personal gain, and history is littered with accounts of second generation failing to have or understand what the previous generation understood and meant.

The voice of God: Real and absolutely necessary to our salvation. If you are not sure you have heard God speak, you need to seek His word, not necessarily an audible utterance, although some have received and heard; rather, that voice that speaks with power in your inmost being. Once you have heard it, you will know it. I am not talking about the low-level utterances that are given in general, but rather a specific word to you, declaring you His child, and at that moment, the Love of God is poured into your heart, the Spirit giving testimony providing assurance, and that will change your life.

Language: Computer-generated translators are breaking down language barriers; it should not be difficult for us to grasp this. The Bible also tells us that at one time, we all spoke the same language. On the day of Pentecost, they all heard Peter's speech in their own language.

Names: Many of the names of the characters appear to be modern names. If you and I were to travel through time and meet many of these people that my character Brea met, would you hear their names in their native language or your language? Many modern names find their origin in ancient times, although modern times may change pronunciation and spelling. The name Talya, for example, while spelled differently, finds its origin in ancient Hebrew. The name Kolby, spelled with a C, can be traced back to the 1100s (the age of the Templars). There is also a secret hidden in many of the names in this book, and only a few will recognize it.

Roman attire and battle gear: Yep, it is all real, taken from history and what we know about the soldiers of that era. The Apostle Paul uses the armor encouraging believers to put it on in his letter to the Ephesians.

Locations: The modern-day cities and towns are real and are around the area where I currently live. However, since all the characters are fictional, so are most of the places they visit, work, and live.

Archeological research and search for sunken ships on the Great Lakes: Real, several have been found, and many are stored in museums in towns surrounding the Great Lakes, do an online search if you would like to visit the museums. Lake Michigan is a very rough lake producing waves as high as twenty feet coming at you from all directions. It has claimed not only ships but countless sailors as well.

That's all for now.
Again, I hope you enjoyed *Pistis the Third Element*.

Printed in the USA
CPSIA information can be obtained
at www.ICGtesting.com
LVHW010721120923
757863LV00008B/134